ABOUT THE AUTHOR

David Griffiths was born and raised in North Wales, before attending the University of Manchester.

He began his teaching career in Stockport and, after a five-year period teaching in Kenya, resumed his UK career in Wilmslow.

He began writing poems, novels and short stories in 1992, but did not attempt to get anything published until recently.

OTHER NOVELS BY DAVID GRIFFITHS
published by Troubador.

Yesterday, Today and Tomorrow
Sharing

David has been shortlisted (top six) for the 2023 King Lear Short Story Prize with *Prisoner 22* and been highly commended in the same competition for *Overcome*.

He has been commended in the Bridport Short Story Competition 2023 for *Nothing There*.

UNRELIABLE MEMORIES

A novel by
DAVID GRIFFITHS

Copyright © 2024 David Griffiths

The moral right of the author has been asserted.

Apart from any fair dealing for the purposes of research or private study, or criticism or review, as permitted under the Copyright, Designs and Patents Act 1988, this publication may only be reproduced, stored or transmitted, in any form or by any means, with the prior permission in writing of the publishers, or in the case of reprographic reproduction in accordance with the terms of licences issued by the Copyright Licensing Agency. Enquiries concerning reproduction outside those terms should be sent to the publishers.

This is a work of fiction. Names, characters, businesses, places, events and incidents are either the products of the author's imagination or used in a fictitious manner. Any resemblance to actual persons, living or dead, or actual events is purely coincidental.

Troubador Publishing Ltd
Unit E2 Airfield Business Park,
Harrison Road, Market Harborough,
Leicestershire LE16 7UL
Tel: 0116 279 2299
Email: books@troubador.co.uk
Web: www.troubador.co.uk

ISBN 978 1 80514 509 7

British Library Cataloguing in Publication Data.
A catalogue record for this book is available from the British Library.

Printed and bound in Great Britain by 4edge Limited
Typeset in 11pt Aldine by Troubador Publishing Ltd, Leicester, UK

"Everybody needs his memories. They keep the wolf of insignificance from the door."

-Saul Bellow, writer, Nobel laureate (1915-2005)

Some memories are clear and seemingly unchanging.
Some survive for only split seconds.
Some come and go, summoned by sounds, smells and images.
Some seem to last forever.
Most will never come back, wiping out patches of our lives.

SUNDAY

I put the suitcases down on the small area where the stairway turned through a right angle, the first upward flight longer than I thought, the cases heavier. Behind me was the foyer in front of the booking kiosk and, away up to the left, the platform, although I could see only the girders supporting the station roof and a strip of sky below it. A youth bounded past me, his heavy-soled shoes catching the metalled edges of the steps with a defiant ring. His coat brushed against mine, but the contact was minimal. He was out onto the platform before I could complain.

I could have bounded like that once – even with these cases. When I was in the army, I could race up hills carrying my full pack and weapons. No problem then. Enjoyed it. Enjoyed being tired. The physical pain, the triumph. Not now. Too many ciggies, too many pints, too many years on the road had taken their toll. Yet I did bound up stairs like those once. Not the stairs in front of me then, but others, up to a railway platform in another station and in another time. No heavy cases then, only a bucket and spade. Off to the seaside. Dad carried the cases, but if he ever stopped under the burden, I didn't see him. I was off and up, carried onwards by the excitement, Mam calling after for me to be careful. He wouldn't have stopped, not Dad, not him who'd fought the Germans and won the war himself, I thought. Mam wouldn't have helped; she was too small. Dad wouldn't have allowed it anyway. Carrying cases was a man's job. She carried her handbag looped over the crook of her arm and a canvas bag with the sandwiches for the journey, warping as the bag pressed them around the Thermos flask full of hot, sweet tea. "Banana sarnies", Dad called them. Bent like a banana they were. But not banana inside – paste or jam more like. How many years ago was that? Thirty? More than thirty! Nearly forty. And how many times did we three do that journey? Such journeys. It seemed throughout my childhood but was probably no more than ten summers. Ten summers! A lifetime of childhood.

But this was no time for reminiscing; I had to press on. Not that there was any rush. My train wasn't due for ages. But I couldn't stand there like a pillock. Some sarky bastard might offer to help. I wasn't having that.

I picked up the cases again, filling my lungs to get the purchase; I felt the muscles pull in my stomach. The front edge of the cases kicked against the steps, and I stumbled forwards under my own momentum. I retrenched on the level elbow of the stair and looked to see if anyone had noticed. There was no one. I paused to take breath and took in the advertisements for trips to Bridlington, Colwyn Bay and London.

Why had I taken so much? I didn't know how long I would be away – might be days – might be weeks. I continued my climb. At last, I reached the top and saw the station spread before me. A long platform in front, and, beyond the tracks, another platform marooned as the metal lines bent either side of it like a fast-flowing stream encountering a boulder. I sought the nearest bench and placed the cases against one end. It was not like the wrought-iron monsters of another age but had a slim, practical design reduced to flimsiness by fashion and finance. I slumped down on it and, by habit, reached for my cigarettes. I paused to let my breathing return to normal and then flicked the wheel of the lighter, leaving the flame to linger before pushing the cigarette into it. I breathed in deeply, the smoke soft and comforting.

The top of the lighter – gold-like but not gold – snapped shut with a sharpness which would catch the attention of bystanders, but there were none close enough to hear. Two benches away sat the youth who had overtaken me on the stairs. When he passed me, he had seemed strong and bulky, a slight threat to my ageing frame. On closer inspection, he was just a lightly built teenager, sitting with his legs stretched in front of him, crossing over at the ankles. In my day, his shoes would have been winkle-pickers. His were stunted and bulky, Doc somethings I think. William had nagged me to buy some.

Beyond the youth sat an elderly couple eating some food from a plastic container. I couldn't see it at first, but they had a Thermos flask perched on the bench between them. A modest suitcase was on the bench alongside the man, and he repeatedly draped his arm protectively over it. It was a bit like the ones we had when we went on holiday as a family, leather with strong stitching around the edges, made to last, and for this couple it had.

They brought back memories of Mam and Dad. These two were somebody's Mam and Dad, I thought. What were their sandwiches today? These two could have been Maureen and me, but how many years hence? Not that many.

It was good to get the weight off my feet. I would not have sat there on those holiday trips but would have raced up and down the platform looking nosily through waiting room windows, peering with disgust into the toilets, swinging around the pillars, the palms of my hands lightly scored by the chipped paint. There seemed so many doors opening onto the platform, most offering a room I was denied entry to. And those into which I was allowed, offered no competition to the excitement of the platform. It was maroon wasn't it – the paint – on the pillars, on the benches, on the waiting room panels. Dull maroon.

There had been a big weighing machine – white face, red surround, much taller than me. When I jumped on its platform, the needle shuddered a little but barely moved from the vertical; my weight was no rival to the parcels and sacks which were its usual clients. And there, between the newspaper kiosk and the long-handled trolleys with their parcels and bundles of newspapers, had been the machine that hammered letters into a metal strip. Into its slot, the first many-edged three-penny bit of my spending money would release the mechanism. I would rotate the stiff finger which pointed in turn to the letters of the alphabet and pulled the stubborn handle until it fell under my effort, slowly at first but then in an easy clanking stroke. One by one, the letters of my name appeared on the aluminium strip. PETER WILFRID CARTER. WILFRID! I wouldn't print that now. My business cards don't say WILFRID. Just Peter Carter. Not even a W in the middle. It's not what the customers want. Nothing fancy. Just Peter Carter. A simple name, a simple guy. You know where you stand with a man with a name like that. You can trust him. That's important when you're selling. Peter W Carter just wouldn't be the same. As though something was being hidden, some sleight of hand to bruise a livelihood. As though the middle name put you into a class above your customers. But WILFRID was all right in those boyhood days. That's who I was – the name in the school register, the name on the tags in my clothes, the name I once scored out in the flattened seaside sand over twenty thousand tides ago only to stand helpless as the incoming waves slowly washed it away. I suppose I was named after somebody, but there was never an Uncle Wilfrid that I recall. A granddad perhaps? But they were long dead when I was born. Perhaps they only lived in photographs, with no names visible, just anonymous men and unknown women, each looking sternly and anxiously out of a sepia mist into a brighter world, leaving later generations free to abandon these strangers to the jumble sale or the dustbin. There might be names on the back of the prints hidden by the stiff card held in place by a gummed paper strip curling as the glue gave up its strength. There they would remain, the ink staying strong and clear, away from the air, identifying the couple by some graffiti, perhaps to be deciphered by an intrigued collector of the fossils of human lives.

I looked at my watch, impatient to get on with my journey.

The metal strip with my name on it had two little holes punched in each end so that it could be tied or pinned to some precious personal item. But it didn't often get that far. Even if I had completed the actions without a spelling mistake, then before the end of the journey it would be bent and twisted by fingers fuelled by the boredom, excitement, indifference, experimentation, anticipation, that flooded my being on those journeys. I never managed to fold it end to end more than twice over. It rarely left the train with me but might lie twisted in some smelly ashtray with my father's dog-ends or tumble to the track through an open window which sucked smell and cinder into our carriage. But I still have my name. It is still me.

A pigeon fluttered down from the girders above me and sat fattening itself on the scraps on the platform, pecking with a seemingly undiscriminating zeal, as though the act of pecking was nourishment enough. It looked like it was wanking. Peck, peck, peck. Wank, wank, wank. Lucky sod, but it was no time to think of that.

It was just like the pigeons of childhood, many generations later of course, but they had not changed, though I wouldn't have thought of wanking then. When an infant, I would have stepped towards it, hesitant because of my size against its. But when older and bolder, I would have advanced confidently, frightening it to fly to its perch above. I flicked my cigarette butt towards it, and it paused to watch it pass, easing its wings from its body as if preparing to escape danger.

We both seemed indifferent to each other's presence. I had an excuse, as four decades had sapped my enthusiasm for the sideshows of everyday life. It could have had no such excuse. I wondered whether birds – perhaps all wildlife – had developed an indifference too, forced by changing human behaviour around them, along an unrelenting urban treadmill. The youth, now leaning against a pillar, shifted his stance, and the sound of his shoe on the platform sent the pigeon skywards.

Despite the large platform clock clicking away the minutes, I kept looking at my watch. This habit of my working life had no point here. There was nothing I could do. Time would pass. The train would come. I would get on it. It would take me on my journey. I would not have to make a decision. I could not influence its arrival. I could not change its direction. I just had to sit, powerless.

A Tannoy gave out a muffled message that only those who knew what to expect could understand. I couldn't understand a bloody word. I stood up and tugged my cases – one at a time – to leave them near the edge of the platform. Something moved at the point where the track wound out of sight. Something of the circumstances of my being there made me expect a whistle and a plume of smoke, to look forward to steam gushing from oily pistons as the train arrived. There were none of these, and the smell was not the sweet aroma of warm grease but the dirty tang of diesel.

Doors opened, but no throng descended on my town, just stragglers in the afternoon lull. I waited while one man came out from my carriage. As I waited, I saw the youth carrying the old couple's suitcase and lifting it up after them.

I heaved my cases into the passageway and got in alongside them. There was no luggage storage bay at my end of the carriage, so I tried to stack them as neatly as I could near the door. I chose a seat which allowed me to see them, but just who would run off with cases I could barely lift I didn't consider. There would be someone to take advantage, wouldn't there? Someone to pull a trick – to beat you to a parking space, to scrape your car and not leave a message, to chuck chip wrappers into your front garden, someone to cancel a long-standing order because they'd got a better deal from some other supplier. Bastards.

I reached for my cigarettes again, only to have a passenger across the aisle cough gently and point to the no-smoking sign above. I could have looked for a smoking compartment, but I couldn't lug all my luggage up the train. I'd just have to put up with it.

It was strange being in a train again, not having to drive, to watch out for other motorists, to take risks. You don't see much of your surroundings when you drive a car. Your thoughts are on the traffic. Your speed too great to allow your mind and eyes to wander. Houses and hedges blot out views of the surrounding area. But you can see an awful lot from a train. Too much in fact.

Who the hell lives alongside a railway line, and have they no shame? Uncut lawns, barking dogs tied to posts, old furniture left to rot. Even the tidy ones are awful: pretentious garden furniture, gnomes. They display their gardens with the same disregard for taste as passengers in an airport lounge display their holiday clothes. But they're exposing themselves like a child with its pants down. Allowing us to see the private parts of their lives usually hidden away behind the covering of their houses.

'Tickets please.'

Where the hell was it? Not in my shirt pocket. Too big for that. It was in my raincoat.

They used to be small way back then. A small, thick card. Solid. Dependable. Collectable. Not now. The inspector took my ticket and returned it with institutionalised deference.

'Thank you, sir.'

Did he enjoy this job, I wondered? Up and down the train; up and down the track. Where was the buzz in that? Why didn't he get a life?

Like *I* have. I am a salesman. Not just any old rep; I am top drawer. Out on the road somewhere different every day. New faces, new places and new products now and again. OK, much of it is repeat business and all the welcome for that. But you're not just selling this batch; you're selling the next one as well – like a snooker player thinking about the best position for the next shot. That's why they've got to trust you, got to like you. And they like Peter Carter. They say you should like the product, but I don't care. It's the selling not the goods that I like. I wouldn't buy some of the stuff I sell; well, I don't have to, of course, that's one of the perks. Then there's the odd bottle of whisky here, the promotion there. And the company looks after their top salesmen, and it's a man's world. I've won a family holiday twice for being top dog in the region. Took Maureen and the kids to Lanzarote the year before last, two-week holiday in a top hotel with five hundred quid in your hand for spending. But you have to earn that kind of thing. Up and down the bloody motorways, different hotel room every other night, and believe you me, some of the hotels make a real bollocks of the simplest meals. How can you spoil steak and chips? I've seen some masters, I can tell you. Still, a couple of pints and a glass of red wine, and all's well with the world. But it's the days that make it worthwhile. Seeing those people sign up for several grand's worth of goods makes my arse go tight. And I shake them by the hand. Thanks very much. And underneath I'm thinking: *I've won*. I get them to do a favour for me, and they think I'm doing a favour for *them*. I have them by the balls, but I don't squeeze; I stroke. I go back to the car, and before I drive off, I light up a fag – especially if the punter isn't a smoker and I've denied myself for an hour or so. I look at the order form and I feel great. There's nothing like it. Well, there is, but that's another story. And that's another thing. Stories. You've got to get the right story for the right customer. Most of them like to think they're a sort of Jack the Lad. Well, they are in a way, because they're selling too; got their hands round somebody else's balls. So, for most of them, they like something a bit naughty, a bit of sex obviously, but nothing kinky, a joke they can tell back at the pub or on the golf course. But you have to be very careful with some. It's not that they haven't got a sense of humour necessarily, but they can be a bit prudish or pretend to be anyway. For them, you can dredge up jokes you've heard on the telly. And the ladies. Ah, the ladies, bless them. No jokes for them. Well, except that Maggie what's-her-name in Stoke. Christ, she knows more than I do. And the things she tells me. No, with the ladies you need a bit of finesse; got to notice what their wearing, cut of their hair and so on. And if you think that's all a bit sexist, you'd be absolutely right, but it works like a dream. But with selling, you don't tell people what they don't want to hear if you want to sell them what they don't want to buy.

A squeal of brakes and a deceleration of the train signalled that we'd arrived. I'd dozed off. I was miles away. I usually *was* miles away.

I bumped the cases onto the platform and looked around. This wasn't just another station. This was where I had bounded up the steps four decades before. This was where I had stamped out my name, but there was no sign of the machine. This was where I had come with Mam and Dad for a simple family holiday. No Lanzarote. Not many coins in my pocket to spend on things I didn't want. Just Mam and Dad and me together. And now I was going home, but not as I had come home then. No sand in my hair, no rubber ball won on a stall, no wondering if the house had changed in those few days away. Now I had come to watch my father die. I didn't want to do it. I'd rather he was already dead than I should sit there with him, both of us knowing the outcome. He might be already dead, dying as I was on my way. The next few days would see no triumphs; I could not expect those spasms of elation that normally fuelled my life. It would be awful, and it was unavoidable. Wilfrid was coming home.

I stumbled down the stairs, the weight of my cases pulling me off balance. I stopped at the foot of the stairs and rested the cases. I didn't turn to look at the steps behind me. I knew they were there. I knew they had been a pathway to sunnier days, innocent days, and I didn't want to be reminded. Through the glass doors of the station approach, I could see the bus shelter. I pushed open the doors with my shoulder and jumped the cases through. There was no taxi in sight, so I stood by the bus stop. A taxi, if one came, a bus otherwise.

I'd spent many an hour on this spot, with Gordon mainly, although sometimes we all came out for a night in town, not wanting to go home, but with no wish to stay after the last bus. But this wasn't the bus shelter of youth. That had been concrete with rusting reinforcing rods exposed where the concrete had broken away under frost and frenzy, and within the concrete frame, wire-enforced glass unyielding to many a missile but crazed in consequence. This one was mostly glass with a simple bench inside. I sat on it and got out my cigarettes. I blew the smoke into the cool late-afternoon air, where it hung for a moment like a megaphone from my mouth before drifting away on the irregular breezes of the traffic. I crumpled the empty packet and threw it towards the litter bin on the bus stop post. I was Peter Carter, top Olympic fag packet thrower. It missed and tottered drunkenly on its crumpled corners into the road.

Gordon and I must have been here many times, tripping off the pavement, bumping into each other and laughing like lunatics, giving the V to honking motorists.

I wondered how Gordon was. I wondered *where* Gordon was. I should look him up. God, I could have killed for a pint. The George was just round the corner. Cross the road, turn right at the laundrette – it wasn't a laundrette then, it was a… what was it now? We wouldn't have noticed as we raced back from the pub to catch that last bus, yet we passed it often enough on our way into town.

It was a gas showroom. That was it.

We pissed through its letterbox once. It was just the right height. Gordon held it open for me and then I did the same for him. Only I let the flap slip and Gordon's piss splashed back all over his pants. Lads, eh.

The George. It would still be there, wouldn't it? They don't close pubs down, do they? Somehow, they hang on. I wondered, was it the same landlord? Couldn't be. He was an old sod then. Seemed old anyway. Couldn't go there. Might have missed my bus. Anyway, I couldn't leave the cases. Some bugger might have nicked them.

The double-decker bus swung round the corner and pulled up at the stop, its wheels crushing my cigarette packet. The driver opened the hinged doors and switched off the engine. He changed the destination screen to read: Fincham via Eldon.

'What time you going?'

The driver looked at his watch. 'About twenty minutes.'

'That long?'

'Are you getting on?'

'What's the chance of a taxi?'

'Where're you going?'

'Eldon.'

'No chance. They'll all be booked for the London train. They won't want to go that far.'

'There might be one dropping someone off.'

'Might be. He shouldn't pick you up anyway. You're supposed to phone them.'

I clamped the ciggie between my teeth and bundled the cases onto the luggage rack beneath the stairs. The exertion made me cough.

'No smoking downstairs, mate.'

'Cheers.'

I went to the back seat of the upper deck just as Gordon and I used to do as teenagers. When younger, I always sought the front seat. I could see the world from there – my little world anyway. Now it looked different but no better. A small town, but a town none the less, with no prospects. I felt glad to have got away. Yet for me it had been the big city, far enough away from home to misbehave. Gordon and me would come here, fancying our chances, fancying ourselves. But it was pathetic. I can see that now. A few beers. Or a picky at the Odeon. Trading soundbites with the local girls. A bag of chips and home on the bus. And we felt great. Sometimes a gang of us would come: Me, Gordon, Bendy, Gary and Howard. I don't know how Howard got in with us. He was much quieter. Had a bit more money than us. First one to get a car, and we used to make him drive us to pubs in the little villages about. We used him really, but he didn't mind. He wanted to be one of us. But he didn't quite fit in. But he was there when Billy died, so he was one of us. We were all tied together by that.

The bus started up and brought me back to the present. I'd ridden the route lots of times since the days when Dad took me to the afternoon pictures, and afterwards, we had fish and chips sitting in the café on Lord Street. We'd always come upstairs on the way back. You could see the world from there, and Dad could smoke. In the dark evenings, the interior lights on the bus reflected off the windows, and I had to press my face to the glass to see out. Mostly there was nothing to see, but I looked just in case there was something worthwhile. Once, when the bus pulled up at the lights on Broad Farm Road, I was level with a window of a flat above a row of shops. The curtains were open and inside I could see a woman opening the front buttons of her blouse, revealing her bra. Before she went further, the bus moved off. I looked in the reflection of the passengers in the bus window and saw Dad looking in the other direction talking with the conductor. The end of his cigarette glowed bright red as he drew breath. I was shocked by what I had seen; it seemed shameless. But it was exciting too and nudged something in me towards puberty and a new view of life. It was nothing to what I've seen since, mind.

When the bus pulled up this time, there was nothing to see. The shops were still there and the windows above, but they offered nothing now but the reflection of the No. 43 and, just briefly, my own outline. I reached in my pocket for a cigarette, but I had none. There were some in one of the cases downstairs.

The bus seemed to pull up at every bus stop whether anyone wanted to get off or not. The sights were still comfortingly familiar in outline, even though they had changed in detail: the big water tower, the hospital set back from the road, a small industrial estate, a large Victorian house built in its own grounds and set back from the main road, its frontage previously a grass lawn, now a tarmacked car park, the sharp bend where the modern road replaced one branch of an old one, the few miles of countryside, a break from drab suburbia, the road signs announcing each village, ticking off stages on my journey home. It had been an easy journey once, my moods reflecting changes in my developing body from childish delight, through youthful indifference, to drunken revelry. It was a sombre trip now.

As we eased towards Eldon I saw, on the opposite side of the road, the first of the row of post-war council houses, one of which had been my family home since I started at the village school. They were semi-detached with front gardens and a grass verge between the footpath and the road. Between each pair was a double driveway with ample room for cars to access standard garages just beyond the building line of the house. This was usually divided by a low fence. The land beyond the houses was long enough to allow substantial gardens. When our houses were first built, these back gardens ended at the fields which marked the countryside beyond, but soon after, those fields had been used to build a larger council estate that robbed our house of its country outlook. By good judgement or miscalculation, some planner had left room for a track to run along the back of our gardens so that the new houses did not overpower us. The first batch, where we lived, had been built to rehouse families, including us, who had previously lived in a run-down terrace up Wellworth Road. Not all the new tenants had come from there; some had been living with parents and presumably reached the top of a housing list. The second batch of houses reached a wider group. Most were existing residents of Eldon, and the new houses were not seen as an intrusion into the community. Gary and Bendy lived there, but I don't recall where they lived before. On my side of the road, newer houses now lined the roadside, blocking out what had in our day been open fields.

We reached my stop, the journey just short of an hour, but it seemed forever. As I got off the bus, struggling with my cases under the indifferent eye of the driver, I was facing the playing fields where I had spent many hours playing football and cricket. A group of about ten boys were playing there in the growing gloom. A thin veil of autumn mist was beginning to come down. The bus obscured my view of the family home. As it drove off, the row of once identical semis was revealed before me. The front gardens were unfenced to begin with, but in time, generations of occupiers had added low hedges, ironwork fences or solid walls, giving a ragged appearance of individualism. Dad had planted a hedge which he cultivated diligently, but now it had grown substantially; even from the other side of the road I could see it needed cutting as small branches overflowed the footpath. It was not yet dark, but most of the houses had their lights on in anticipation of the gloom. Our house was the right-hand one of a pair of semis about fifty yards down the road, and I knew all the others from my childhood. Opposite the bus stop had lived the Gartsides, probably not now, they seemed old then, though they had a daughter, a bit older than me. Annette. Gordon said he'd had it with her, but nobody believed him. She wasn't much of a looker, so it wasn't something to brag about anyway. She had an older brother and sister who lived away. I crossed the road towards their house before turning towards ours. Who the hell lived joined to them? The gate was hanging off and the privet hedge had grown high and straggly. Then Mrs Bescott. Then attached to it, Gordon's house. Then ours, separated from Gordon's by a low fence.

Ours? It wasn't mine anymore. I'd grown away from it. It was Mam and Dad's. I looked up at the front bedroom window. Theirs. There was a low light in it. The hall light was on, and I could see the kitchen light shining onto the path where Gordon and I had kicked a football, had our fights, mended our bikes and, as we got older, took out our fags as we walked to the bus, announcing our coming with loud talk and puffs of smoke. I didn't want to go in. I feared what I'd find. I'd find Dad. Not the strong, wiry man I had admired but a weakened shell, breathing out his last in a smelly bed. I had not yet seen him, but I could guess. I supposed he would be able to talk. And perhaps that would be worse. Perhaps I could cope with Dad as a corpse but not a living, withered, failing, conscious person. Did I really hope he had already died?

I went to the back door. Where else? I wasn't a visitor. I saw my mother through the kitchen window before she saw me. Hardly changed, it seemed. Her hair shaped to her head as always, grey now, but it had always seemed subdued. Her brown-framed glasses had slipped to the end of her nose as she bent over the sink. She looked up as my movement flicked a reflection into the kitchen. There was a brief flash of brightness in her face which made me feel good to be back, but her face never had been full of life. There was a steadiness, a certainty about her personality which had always made my childhood safe. No theatricals, no temper, no tears even when I did the most awful things that children do, these not the same as the awful things adults do. I wondered what she would make of *them*.

She opened the door and pulled it wide. 'Hello, Peter. It's nice to see you. Thanks for coming. Come in.'

I couldn't reply. I knew there were tears in my eyes, not those that roll with salt but those that sting with pepper. I reached for her, not her for me, but she came into my embrace.

'How is he?'

'So-so.'

'I'd better go up to see him. Is he awake?'

'I don't know. Bring your cases up.'

She didn't need to say I was in my old room, a room that once hung with model aeroplanes and now saw only the framed photos of a childhood. I put down the cases alongside the bed and waited on the landing.

Mam came out of the front bedroom. 'He's a little drowsy. Come in.'

I didn't want to go in. I would have given anything to avoid that first encounter. There would be nothing in that room I could enjoy. There was no future in there, and the decaying present would only sully the past. It could not be avoided, and I went in. The sour smell came before I edged past the door. I saw the end of the bed first, his feet raising the crocheted cover above the sheets like tumbledown drawbridge towers at the entrance to a castle, like the ones we had built at the seaside many times and many years ago. More and more his form grew until I saw his face lying deep within the pillow. So deep had he sunk into it, that the light from the bedside lamp threw a shadow across his face so that only his nose was lit. It took me a while to recognise him. The eyes and mouth, those things that had given him vitality, were sucked into a withered skin, leaving his nose a bony protuberance above the pillow. His false teeth were in a glass tumbler beside his bed. They were facing me as they would in his mouth. My mother moved to close the curtains, leaving me alone by the bed.

'Hello, Dad.' I didn't know I had such softness in my voice, he the child now. 'How are you feeling?'

His eyes had been closed, but they eased open at the sound of my voice.

'Hello, Peter. I'm OK. Mustn't grumble.' He smiled, the routine smile of greeting, but not the sure smile of contentment.

I didn't know what to say next. No place for honesty now, only the half-truths that would prevent hurt.

'I took the bus. Couldn't get a taxi.' It seemed so inadequate.

I couldn't tell whether he'd heard what I said so didn't know whether to carry on.

Mam appeared and said, 'He's gone back to sleep. You unpack, and I'll make you a nice cup of tea.' As she ushered me out of the room, I glanced towards the bed and saw his false teeth grinning back, the only sign of life left.

I was surprised how small my old bedroom seemed. Little had changed, the single bed alongside the inner wall and a dark wood wardrobe opposite it. I knew that on the end of the dressing table, hidden against a wall, were my initials, scratched there when I was thirteen or fourteen for no good reason I could recall other than to fill an idle wet afternoon. Perhaps I was subconsciously trying to leave a mark on life to survive me when I'd gone, but I don't suppose I saw it that way. PWC, Wilfrid lives on.

I unpacked, putting my clothes in the drawers and hanging spaces that had once contained their smaller predecessors. I caught sight of myself in the mirror on the dressing table. I didn't look good; I didn't feel good. My face was full, perhaps a little too full, not like Dad's. And it was florid, another sign of good living, whereas Dad's had lost all pretence of colour. He would have looked in mirrors and seen his lively, confident face looking back – not now, no more now. I bet when he first wore his army uniform, he stood there weighing himself up. I did. Turning my body from one side to the other, pushing out my chest and holding in my stomach. It certainly needed holding in now.

I put the cases, now empty and easy to lift, on top of the wardrobe and made to go downstairs. I paused on the landing and listened for sounds from the front bedroom. There were none. No uniforms in there; just an old soldier in a rearguard action. I didn't want to peer round the door so trod stealthily down the stairs.

Mam was in the back room, a teapot in hand. The room had not changed, though it now seemed smaller, furniture dark but polished, the same pictures on the wall.

'It's just ready. Do you want sugar?'

'Just one.'

'So many young people seem to do without these days.'

Did she still class me as young?

'How are you coping?'

'I'm all right. It's a bit lonely at times. He doesn't say much.'

'I should have come before. I didn't realise how bad he was.'

'We didn't want to bother you. You've got your own family… how's Maureen?'

'She's fine. Enjoys her job.' The money's handy.

'And William. Has he got a job yet?'

'No. Says he's waiting for the right opening.' Idle little sod. I could've got him a job at our warehouse. All he had to do was turn up. But, oh no, not him. Wanted time to sort out his future, he said. He needn't think he's sponging on me.

'And what about Claire? She's got exams soon, hasn't she? Is she going to stay on at school?'

'No, she wants to go to college. Nursery nursing or something.'

'That's nice.'

No money in that. What a pair. Neither of them wants to get out and graft. They're going to be looking to me for money I expect.

I worked the moment I left school. Well, that and college once a week as well. I can recollect opening that wage packet, one of those buff ones with the deductions written on the pre-printed panel. Four pounds something. I can remember peeling back the self-gummed flap and pouring the coins into my hand. I squeezed them. Then I took out the notes and counted them out. I gave Mam two when I got home. It was what was expected then. Not now it seems.

I reached for the new packet of cigarettes from my jacket pocket.

'I'd rather you didn't smoke here, Peter. Not in the house.'

Not smoke! We'd always smoked. Me and Dad. Specially him. Hardly ever without a fag in his mouth. When he came back from the war, there he was, coming down the steps of the bus, a fag clamped in his mouth. But he couldn't hold a cigarette now. Couldn't draw breath to take in the smoke.

'I'm sorry. It's habit I'm afraid. How long has he been like this? You didn't say anything.'

'I suppose it's been coming on for a while. You don't notice. It works so slowly.'

It! The big C. Neither of us could say it.

'I've not spoken to him for ages. It was always you on the phone. You always said he was busy.'

'Well, he didn't want to bother you. I think he's

known for some time but said nothing. He used to go to the hospital in Cooksley. Used to tell me it was something to do with his pension. Health check. You know.'

'If I'd have known, I'd have driven over. It's only a couple of hours.'

'Why didn't you drive today?'

She had to know sometime.

'I've been banned. Speeding. I've lost my license for a while.' Speeding and some. Well over the limit more like. Double they said. But that was bollocks. *And not the first time, Mr Carter.* Bloody magistrate. Pompous twat. Got away with a year though. I pleaded it was my job. I have to travel to do my job. I was lucky. No two ways about it. Lucky with the firm too. They've put me in head office until I get my license back. But they know where their bread's buttered. I'm their top salesman. Lose me and they lose a big slice of business. I can still do more selling over the phone than some of the other dickheads do out on the ground. Still, not having a car has been a real pain.

'Oh dear. It's lucky Maureen can drive. There was no point in me learning to drive. With us not having a car.'

'Yeah. She'd have run me over here in hers, but she's working today. She dropped me at the station.'

'That's nice.'

Nice. So she bloody should. Who paid for the car anyway? Took all my annual bonus, did that. No big holiday that year.

'It must be hard work for you, looking after him. Do you get any help?'

'The nurse comes every day. She helps me wash him.'

The thought of Dad being washed by a strange woman upset me. They'd wash him all over, wouldn't they? They'd have to. All over!

'Do you get enough rest?'

'Yes, he's under a lot of drugs.'

'And at night?'

'He wakes now and then. Wants a drink usually. I don't often have to get up.'

So, she was lying there each night in the same bed as a dying man! Still, they'd always slept together in that big, iron-framed bed with old-fashioned mattress. No duvet. Sheets and a quilt for them.

'Do you get out much?'

'Not a lot. Freda next door does some shopping for me. I miss the church on a Sunday, but Mr Baverstock comes in to see me every couple of days. He's nice. You've never met him, have you?'

I've never met any of the bloody vicars, not since I left school anyway. Never been near the church. Nor Dad. Mam has. Every Sunday morning without fail. Does the flowers once a month. Social meeting in the week. Christ knows what she sees in it.

'Well, you can get out a bit now I'm here.'

I'd be alone in the house with Dad! I wasn't going to wash him. Suppose he died when she was out. I wondered whether he'd want a chat. We could talk about the days out to the pickies. And repairing the bike tyres. And working in the shed with all those tools. And gardening over at Auntie Pauline's. And sitting at the end of our garden having a fag. Both of us. Talking about the war. And once he talked about his mate being killed. Auntie Pauline's husband. What the hell was his name? And sometimes Gordon would be there, and he'd have a fag as well, as long as his mam and dad didn't find out. Gordon wasn't there when Dad talked about… what was his name now? There was usually just the two of us.

'That would be nice. Just for a change.'

'What was Dad's friend called? The one who got killed in the war. Auntie Pauline's husband.'

'His name was Harry. Harry Dobson.'

'Did you know him?'

'Yes. The four of us were best friends before the war. And Harry and Dad went off to war together.'

'And was Auntie Pauline there too?'

'Yes, she was.'

'So did she ever see him alive again?'

'Yes. He came home on leave to get married just before he was killed.'

'That must have been hard for her.'

'Yes, the two of us were very close until Dad came back from the war and things changed a bit.'

'I suppose you had me to look after.'

She brought the conversation to an end. 'I'll just go and get tea ready. I've got some chops. Pork. You like them, don't you? It'll be a bit strange cooking for two again.'

'Can I do anything?'

'No, you sit and watch the telly. There's some news coming up. The paper's over there if you want it.'

There must have been a time when I saw that room

as mine. Well, ours anyway. Our family's. Where our lives overlapped. Yet now I felt a stranger. The wallpaper, the ornaments, the curtains, all seemed not just of another time but another world. I thought I had grown away from it, out of it. But there I was sitting in it again. Mam in the kitchen. Dad somewhere about the house. I'd slipped back into it. It was reclaiming me, and I felt frightened. I went to the kitchen.

'All right if I smoke outside?'

'If you must.'

And I had to.

MONDAY

I awoke convinced I hadn't slept. I couldn't get to sleep, I thought. A strange bed, a house colder than I was used to even though it was barely autumn. I lay under the sheets trying to gather the courage to get up.

I would have died for a pint last night, but I couldn't leave Mam. She had some sherry in. I could see it in the front room cabinet. But she didn't offer any. Thank God. Sherry! But I must have slept. But no alcohol. A whole day with no alcohol. When did that last happen?

I looked at the bedside clock. It was a quarter to nine. I must have slept. I wondered how Dad was. Was he still alive? There'd be a commotion if he'd gone, surely. Mam would be crying, and I would have heard her. I would have heard her, wouldn't I? She would have cried, wouldn't she?

I reached out to touch the radiator. It was cold. October and no heating on! There was no radiator when this was my room, not 'til I left home. I used to sit on the windowsill and kick my heels against the plaster. And kneel on the sill and stretch my body out through the open casement as far as I could go without falling. I slipped once. Just grabbed the frame in time. Jabbed my ribs on the window stay as I fell. I can feel that sudden pulse in my heart now. I felt good afterwards. I'd taken a risk. All right, a small, pathetic, schoolboy risk. And I'd survived. I wore the bruise on my ribs with pride but didn't notice its going. Life is like that. Brushing away the little injuries and letting you get on with it. The little things, that is. The bigger things hang around waiting to be recalled until some idle thought pushes them out front – usually when you want them forgotten.

Getting up, I pulled on my dressing gown and headed for the bathroom. There was a noise downstairs in the kitchen. I edged into the front bedroom. My washbag caught the edge of the door, making a slight noise, and Dad opened his eyes.

'Hello, Peter. I didn't know you were here.' What had happened to the previous day?

'Thought I better check how you were getting on.'

His arms were outside the bedclothes. I wanted to touch him, but his hands were thin, brittle enough to break. And they weren't the hands I knew. Hands that held me high. Hands that ruffled my hair. Hands that guided mine when he taught me how to hold a saw. Hands that formed a cage for his cigarette. I wondered about the tattoo on his right forearm, some badge I never understood what. Would that now be shrivelled with his wrinkled skin? Of course, it would. A tattoo. A permanent statement. A real symbol of a military man. I was in the army too just like Dad. Well, not the same. Just national service. I didn't fight a war – too late for

Malaya, didn't get to Cyprus. Did some fighting though. In the pubs and down the alleys. Daft really, but that's how it is when you're young and cocky. They were good days. You felt you were pushing yourself, real physical pain. Making a man of yourself. And the uniform. Did that pull the birds or what? I'll say it did. Scrubbers mainly, but you had a choice. And now and again there was a bit of class.

Dad started to say something else, but his voice trailed off. I suppose he was asleep. Wherever he was, he was not with me. I was losing him and could do nothing about it.

'That was good, Mam. You haven't lost your knack with the food then.'

I like a cooked breakfast when I'm away. Sets me up for the day. Don't eat much at lunchtime. Pint and a sandwich usually. But I do take care with the breakfast. I think the waitresses like it when someone has a full breakfast. It makes their job seem a bit special. I expect some of the older ones think of you as a sort of son who they're looking after. They like a bit of a joke, ask you where you're going and if you're in tomorrow. The younger ones aren't so friendly. Probably thinking of their kids at home messing up the kitchen or lying in bed instead of getting off to school. Nice-looking, some of them. Wearing uniform of course, but not like a nurse. Can't get horny over a light blue overall with splashes of fruit juice on it, can you? Well, not with a plateful of bacon and eggs in front of you.

I pushed the plate away and drew the cup and saucer

in front of me. The tea in the pot was still warm, so I had a second cup. I could see why Mam used a tea cosy, but it was a bit old-fashioned. But then she *was* a bit old-fashioned; old-fashioned values, so I suppose I should have been glad of that. I wanted a fag. You used to be able to have a fag after breakfast in the hotels, but most of them have put a stop to that now. I saw one bloke got really stroppy with a waitress once because she asked him not to smoke. When she came over to my table, to take my order, I put her hand in mine and patted it. I got an extra egg when the plate arrived.

'Shall I wash up?'

'No, I'll do it. I know where everything goes.'

'What's the routine today then?'

'I'd like to go down to the supermarket at about ten. I'll get something nice for tonight. A bit of fish?'

'Yeah. Fine. What do you want me to do?'

'There's not much to do. Look in on him from time to time. You won't hear him call; he's too weak. He'll only want some water. He's had his pills. Dr Jamieson is coming between eleven and twelve, but I'll be back by then.'

It hadn't occurred to me how much time I would have on my hands. I hadn't brought anything to read; I'm not much of a reader anyway. I looked in the paper at the TV programmes. Not much there, but if I could summon up an interest in holidays in Jamaica, vegetarian cooking and Alan Ladd, I might fill up the day somehow. There was no sound from upstairs, and when I did look, there was no movement. I can't say I was sorry.

I wandered around the house and saw the pieces that

were fresh and new in my youth, now worn and stained with the smoke from my father's cigarettes. There was a china dog which surely had both ears intact but now did not. The wallpaper must have been new but looked as though it had been there forever, perhaps once fashionable and warm, but now diminishing the room. These rooms where once I floated paper planes and ran lines of railway track, could now be measured by a few paces. It was as though the fabric of my childhood home had contracted and withered like the skin on my father's hands.

★★★

Dr Jamieson came and went. He was younger than me but had seen much more.

'What did he say?' I asked Mam.

'No real change. He says it will happen quickly when the time comes.'

'How long does he think?'

'He doesn't know.'

Doesn't know or won't say?

'He can't last much longer, can he?'

'No. He's very weak.'

'What will you do... after?'

'Just as I've always done. This is my home. But there'll be plenty of time to think about that.'

'But you'll be all alone.'

'I'll get used to it. You'd be surprised what people get used to. I've got the church. They need volunteers for all sorts of things. Bring-and-buy sales. They're thinking of starting a nursery. Mr Baverstock's got lots of ideas. No, I'll be all right. What about you?'

'Well, I've got Maureen and the kids. And my job. It won't make any difference to me.'

I shouldn't have said that. I didn't mean it. Of course, it will make a difference. Dad won't be here anymore. I haven't seen much of him lately, I know. But I knew he was always there, cutting the hedges, keeping the grass verge at the front tidy even though it's the council's job, popping down to the British Legion for a jar and a natter, cycling over to Auntie Pauline's to keep her garden in shape and do odd jobs. Except he hadn't done these things for some time now; he'd been lying upstairs, dying. Dad was a good father, knew how to treat a son. Strong, helpful, jokey, reliable. None of these things now. I remember when he came back from the war. Sunburnt, upright, comforting. He gave me a good solid home life, ever there, ever strong, ever honest. He and Mam together.

'I'll get some dinner. Beans on toast I thought.'

'Great.' And I meant it.

'Do you think you could cut the hedges this afternoon?'

'Yeah. No problem.' I'd be doing it for Dad.

★★★

It was more a problem than I thought. No power clippers for Dad. Good old-fashioned shears, sharp but stiff. My arms ached, and not just at the end of the day but for days afterwards. My waist was stiff with bending.

My hands had blisters like three-penny bits. Dad used to say that: blisters like three-penny bits. Even the light engine oil didn't help – with the shears, not my blisters. It was easy to find. The shed was laid out with military precision. Every tool in its rack, the work bench clear of shavings. But there was a layer of dust everywhere, and the tenon saw had a hint of rust. Dad would have hated that, but how long had it been since he was in here? We'd spent hours in that shed, a garage for everyone else in the road, but we never got round to a car. Never had the money I suppose. Worked all his life at the joiner's shop on the small estate by the river. Never wanted more, and I suppose old Bennett took advantage of him. Paid him peanuts, so he couldn't afford a car. But I never heard Dad say one word against him.

I'm bloody sure I would have. I'd want to be paid what I'm worth. That's why I've got a car – two cars. That's why I have a good holiday every year, not stuck in a shed like this. What I am saying is: it was magic, this shed. The things we did: drilling, shaping, sawing, soldering. I took all the exams at school – woodwork, metalwork – and then started at college. It was then I realised I was on track for the same life as Dad: small town enterprise paying peanuts because you liked what you were doing. Not for me. So, I was dead pleased when the call-up papers arrived. They saved me from a life like Dad. But Dad had a happy life, didn't he?

Didn't he?

It was strange cutting the front hedge. People kept passing and saying how nice it was to see me again and asking how Dad was. I told them he was OK, but everyone knew he wasn't. They knew me, and I couldn't remember *them*. They'd changed, and I hadn't. No, that's nonsense. I had changed. I was older. I was fatter. OK, OK, I was a bit overweight. And I'd changed inside, though they couldn't see that. They only knew me because I was cutting Dad's hedge. One woman stood for several minutes chatting. I had to pretend I knew her. Couldn't ask about family in case she didn't have any. She hadn't gone more than twenty yards when I recollected who she was. Two kids. A boy older than me who used to deliver our papers. And a girl. Younger. A real cracker. You didn't notice her 'til she got near fifteen or sixteen and then – whoomph – there she was, all tits and lipstick. She played hard to get though. Not even Gordon could pretend he'd got anywhere. Stuck-up bitch.

After I'd done the back garden hedges, I put the shears away in their little rack. Coming out, I caught my shin on Dad's bike. He'd had that all the time I'd known him. A solid upright black number. With a shelf over the back wheel, I think we called it the pillion. I used to sit on that when we went up to Auntie Pauline's to do her garden. Only for a while. I got too old for going with Dad and too big to ride on the back. He still went though. Every Sunday morning while Mam was at church, pushing off from the curb, looking over his shoulder to see there was no traffic, swinging his leg over and pushing steadily 'til he got up speed. It took him all over, that bike: work in the morning, the Legion at Saturday lunchtime, Auntie Pauline's on Sunday morning, then back for one of Mam's Sunday roasts. These places were all in walking distance, but he still took his bike, as though he was saying he was leaving his home and going somewhere different – the people were different; the sounds were different; the rooms were different. I knew what he meant. When I set off on one of my routes, I knew I was going somewhere very different, where the norms didn't apply. Otherwise, life was one long drudge. But I was leaving family life behind. Did you feel that, Dad?

When I came in, Mam made me a cup of tea and my hand shook as I held it, so much did my arms ache.

'Thanks, Peter. It's a job well done. I might be OK for the winter now. I've been paying a lad from down the road to do it.'

'You should've told me. I'd have paid him to do it as well.'

'You look a bit hot and bothered. Look at the sweat under your arms.'

'I'll go and have a bath in a while.'

'I'll go and put the emersion on for the hot water.'

Had the bath shrunk too? Before, there had been room to sail boats and shoot the soap out of my hands at them. Now I barely fitted, and the water lapped perilously close to the top. It was the same bath, but its surface was no longer smooth and shiny, now matt after decades of cleaning. The taps were bulbous and stiff, but it was nice to turn them on again; they filled your hand with strong, smooth metal. When I left home, the bath had been free-standing, with wrought-iron legs. They were hidden now, where Dad – it must have been Dad – had boxed the bath in. No hardboard sheet on wooden frame but neatly cut tongue-and-groove staves butted firmly together with no space between them for dirt and soapy water to accumulate. Such a solid job, so finely done.

I looked in on Dad as I went to dress. No change since this morning. No change that I could see, but I suppose the tightening of the skin was a loosening on life. And those hands that once held such skill, now like claws on a Christmas turkey. I reached down and touched one, stroking the back of it. It was cold against my podgy bath-warm skin, and it retracted, recoiled, I thought. Which just showed how inhuman Dad had become, for in full life he would not have rejected me.

'He's quiet,' I said, when I went to the kitchen.

'I fed him a while ago, and he usually sleeps afterwards. I told him you were doing the hedge. I think he could hear the clippers. He smiled at that. He said something about wiping the blades with an oily rag before you put them away.'

'I'll go and do it now.'

When I came back in, I stood against the sink unit, looking at next door. 'Does anybody hear anything of the Smiths?'

'No. When they won that money – some people say it was a million pounds. I can't believe that, can you? Any big sum of money becomes a million pounds in the telling, doesn't it? It doesn't take much round here to start a rumour. Anyway, once they got the money, they went almost straight away. Gordon too. When Freda moved in, there were no letters piled up. They must have arranged for them to be sent on. But there was no forwarding address. You know like some people leave a card on the mantelpiece. Although, for years, one Christmas card kept arriving here. It had their name on it, but the house number was ours not theirs, so I suppose it got through the net. Freda propped it on the hall windowsill not knowing what to do. Around about March she decided to open it. It was from a couple called Beatrice and Tommy – no real message – season's greetings type of thing. So, in later years, she opened it straight away and put it on her mantelpiece with her own. It seemed a Christmasy thing to do. Nice cards they were – not cheap – charity – Oxfam, I think. Anyway, it went with the others to be recycled at church. We sort them out and those that could be made into pictures we send on. I don't know where they go. Mr Baverstock deals with it.'

I only wanted to know where the family was. How do they do it? Women. They take a little story, and they tell you every blooming detail. As if I cared a toss about Beatrice and Tommy.

'I thought I'd go out tonight, Mam. If that's all right. I might go down to The Anchor just to see if there's anyone I know.'

Might go down to The Anchor indeed. Where else was there to go? Apart from The Church Inn, but that was a bit posh. There was the Legion, but that was full of ghosts. What else to do? To stand at the junction and watch the lorries go by, to lean over the bridge and watch the stream washing against the supports, to walk up to the brow of Leaden Hill and see the lights across the valley. Not likely. Those were trips of long ago. Now I needed a pint.

'Here's a set of keys. In case you're late.'

'I won't be late.' How often had I said that over the years?

'Come in the front door. I won't sleep until you come in.'

'Mam! I'm grown up now.'

'It's not you; it's me. I need to know *I'm* safe. I'll leave the hall light on.'

'I'll be quiet.'

'Good lad.'

★★★

The journey was a familiar one; Gordon and I had done it many times. Across the road, turn right at the postbox, walk fifty yards until the bend in the road allowed us to see any oncoming traffic, diagonally across and onto the pavement outside the newsagents – except it was a chip shop now – and then on the inside elbow of the bend down a narrow street – what was its name? We didn't need to know its name, one-way now – and there it was on the right-hand side of the road, The Anchor.

The Anchor! And so far from the sea. No step, no hanging sign, just a frontage, two large opaque windows separated by a double door into a small entrance hall. Surely the paint work was the same colour it always was? The lounge bar to the left was where the youngsters went. It had a jukebox and a pool table. Gordon and I occasionally went there. Didn't want that now, just a bit of quiet. I went in and through to the right, the bar on my left facing the window, the L-shaped room turning away to the toilets near the back of the pub. At the far end were four men sat around a low table, laughing and joking. One looked across at me, but I didn't recognise him. I nodded just to be friendly. Two youths were leaning on the bar flicking cigarette ash into a logoed ashtray. Just like me and Gordon, back then.

In the corner elbow sat a married couple; I assumed they were married as they didn't speak much. He had a half-empty pint glass in front of him, and she had a half of what looked like lager. There was an open packet of crisps which they were sharing. It was as though, after decades of passing words between each other, they were left with only the sounds of the crunching of crisps. You're a cynical bugger, Peter, and no mistake. But seeing this couple, I remembered I hadn't rung Maureen.

I guessed all the customers were local; they seemed at ease here, not looking around at the horse brasses on the walls or the beer mats tucked into the picture rail. All content, I wondered?

'A pint of Wallbrooks bitter, please.'

Not the same landlord, if indeed this was the landlord. Looked too young. They all do now. A man wouldn't work for what they get paid. Cyril would have retired now, surely. And Joyce. She was all right, Joyce. She was in the right job. Loved what she was doing. Made every customer seem interesting. Always chatting and joking. Even when we were young. Made us feel grown-up. We thought we were grown-up too. Been drinking since we were sixteen. Not here of course. You don't shit on your own doorstep. That's when we started in The Farmers Arms at Fincham. But Joyce seemed to belong here. It was her life I suppose, as good as any other. I don't suppose Cyril was a barrel of laughs. I wondered, did she still do herself up with that lipstick and nail polish? She's probably sat in the corner of some old folk's home decorated like a Christmas tree chatting up the visitors.

'Don't make that anymore, mate. Taken over long ago.'

'Pint of that then.' I pointed to the nearest pump. It didn't really matter anymore.

'Hello, Peter.'

I was taking my first sip, and the words made me spill some out. I turned to face the voice that came from behind me. 'Howard! Bugger me.'

'No thanks. I'd never live it down.'

He was sitting in a corner made by the street wall and the frame of the porch. He was reading a newspaper, or was until I arrived. He looked as though he had always sat there. Like me, he was fatter, but whereas I kept my hair short and businesslike – I was in business after all – he wore his longer and curly. I went to sit next to him, putting my drink on the table before him.

'So, how are you doing? Still working for your dad?'

Although his father was a farmer, he had made a lot of money when he found a lucrative market for the stone from the quarry on the edge of their farmland, just where the valley shaded into Leaden Hill. The stone from it was just the right specification to serve as the base layer of the new road network in the region. All he had to do was fill up a few trucks and drop it where it was required.

'I run the farm. Father died only last year determined to make all the major decisions about the farm, leaving me to deal with the day-to-day running, but he'd stopped work before that. Well, physical work anyway.'

'The quarry's still there?'

'Sure is. Turns over a tidy penny or two.'

'Penny or two! Come off it.'

I was jealous of the bastard, I couldn't deny it. He was rich, and he was lucky. Still, he was a mate. Least he was then. He wasn't quite the same as the rest of us – me, Gordon, Gary and Bendy. But he was always with us. The famous five. Once we were six. Didn't drink as much as us, didn't Howard. Always bought his round, but was usually only halfway through a pint when we left to move on. He didn't swig it down as we would have done. He was rich enough to leave some beer in his glass. Didn't go in for the girls much either; nothing wrong with him mind, never hinted at anything bent. But he wasn't a hunter like the rest.

'Sorry about your father,' Howard said, sympathetically.

'You heard?'

'Everyone hears everything here. I haven't seen your mum for a while, but my mother was talking to someone who told *her*. There's plenty of room for gossip in Eldon.'

'No, Mam doesn't get out so much now.'

'She's well though?'

'Yes, she's fine in herself but has to look after the old feller.'

'How is he?'

'Can't last much longer.'

There was a pause in the conversation.

'I'm sorry. Father went very quickly. He was on the toilet when he had a heart attack. Must have strained with constipation or something. Not the kind of thing to put in the obituary.'

'Or on the gravestone. Is he buried up the road?'

'No, he wanted to be buried at Lower Calton where his parents are.'

Buried with his parents! Would I be buried here? Forever in Eldon when I've tried to escape.

'Understandable I suppose.'

We both paused to drink, he sipping, me a mouthful. He was all right, Howard. A bit odd to look at. I think his legs were too long for his body. But he didn't take himself too seriously.

'Family OK?'

'Yeah. Fine. Maureen's working again so it brings in a bit of money. You married?'

'No. It's not for me. I don't lack for company. Mother's still at the farm. I'm in here most nights. Just a couple of pints usually. I drive down and then get a taxi back if I have too much.'

'Do you ever hear from Gordon?'

'No.'

'Nor me. Not even a card. I was a bit upset by that. He was my best man after all. Strange, isn't it?'

'Once his folks won that money and moved away, he just disappeared. I was a bit miffed really because we spent a lot of time together as lads. Do you remember when we put that toy rabbit down in one of our fields – the one up against Parry's Wood – and bet Gordon he couldn't catch it by throwing his coat over it, watched him squirming along the grass missing the cow pats and then – whoosh – pouncing on this bloody toy rabbit. It was really funny.'

'I expect it was funny, Howard, but it wasn't Gordon; it was me. It was me who made myself look a right prick just to amuse you lot.'

'Sorry, Peter. Yes, you're right. But we were so close you mix things up.'

'For weeks after you were singing: *Run rabbit, run rabbit, run, run, run.*'

'Well, it didn't take much to make us laugh.'

'Do you remember when we pinned that picture of a starlet in a bikini on the church noticeboard?'

'It all seems pretty tame, now.'

'Certainly does… any news about Bendy?'

'He does long-distance driving – for the grain company. Saw him last year sometime. I was at a barbecue. Some charity thing. He seemed OK. Wasn't with his wife. I didn't like to ask. Not my business really.'

'Odd that, cos he was the first to get hitched. You remember he courted that girl from Tarvell, Pat something or other. Wouldn't let us near her.'

'I could get hold of him through the grain company. We could have a pint. Just for old times' sake. And Gary. He still lives locally. Four kids. Got his own business. Painting and decorating. I've got his business card somewhere, stuck in the frame of a mirror at home I expect. The four of us could meet up. Have a meal perhaps. The Farmers at Fincham does food now. All four of us would be good, so many memories.'

I looked away from him, scared of what he might say next. If he caught my eye, he'd know I was thinking of Billy. And I would know he was too. I saw his reflection in the mirror behind the optics. He was looking down, folding his newspaper. I looked back.

'Yeah. Good idea, Howard. You do that. I'm going to be free most nights. Fancy another?'

TUESDAY

'Dear Lord. Please grant Eric the strength to fight the pain of his dreadful illness. Comfort him and guide him through this dark vale and help him see the brightness of your kingdom. Amen.'

'Amen.'

'Amen.'

I was slower to reply than my mother and was left to respond on my own. Throughout the short prayer, I had held my hands together in front of me, like a footballer covering his balls at a free kick, but couldn't bring myself to close my eyes. I felt railroaded into a ceremony in which I couldn't engage. And neither could Dad. Eric, indeed. He was Dad to both of us.

But Mam was serious. She held her hands like a mantis, and her Amen was as full of sincerity as mine was barren of respect. Mr Baverstock smiled wanly at me.

'It's a great strength to your mother for you to be here. I'm so glad you could come.'

'I'd have come sooner, but I didn't know.' Bugger it. He made me feel guilty. But I really didn't know.

'We're having a prayer meeting this evening, Mrs Carter. Do you think you could come? We're having a visitor from our sister church in Tanzania.'

'Well, I'm not sure if I can get away.'

'You go, Mam. I'll cope here.' The guilt was having an effect.

'Oh good. We'll see you about seven-thirty. Goodbye now, and God be with you all.'

Mam took him to the door, and I stood until he'd gone from sight. I cleared away the cups and saucers.

'Thank you, Peter. I would like to go. It's been so long since I've been out in the evening.'

'Since I'm in this evening I'll pop out for a pint after lunch. OK?' I couldn't have stood a whole day in the house.

'OK, love.'

★★★

There was only one other customer. She was sitting at the end of the short bar where I'd ordered my beer. I'd nodded when I'd come in, and she'd smiled back. She was well dressed – a tight-fitting black suit, skirt pulled up as her crossed legs pointed towards me. Her white blouse seemed to hide a comfortable body beneath. Her blonde hair – dyed surely – seemed stiff as it coiled around her face, its bright lipstick matching her nail varnish. This was crumpet with a capital K. I lit up a cigarette and placed the lighter on top of the packet on the bar.

'Have you got a light?' She leaned forwards, a

tipped cigarette in her right hand. She'd had a bit too much to drink, judging by the way she tried to show she hadn't.

Had I got a light? What did she think I lit my fag with, a flame-thrower? And what was that on the bar, a bloody Christmas tree decoration? Of course, I'd got a light for her. I felt I was in there. This was a cert, a traveller's bonus if ever I saw one.

I can't explain what I was thinking then. A crude lust had taken over, powered by what? Not just alcohol. It had got me in difficulties before. I don't suppose it would have made much difference even if my mind had intervened.

'Yeah. Sure.' I eased over and struck the lighter. I was trying to remember to hold in my stomach. I held one hand over hers to bring the cigarette and light together. As she put the end of the cigarette into the flame, her eyes caught mine. I knew what she was thinking, and she was one hundred per cent right.

'I haven't seen you here before.'

'Just a flying visit. Family. Parents.' I shouldn't have said *family*; it begs too many questions. Not that she wanted to ask them.

'Local, are you?'

'I was once. Not anymore.' I was. I was a boy here once. In this very bar. But I wasn't a boy anymore. I was a man now. She'd see.

'Where do you live now?'

'Near Manchester. Out towards the Pennines.' That was far enough away. No complications.

'I've got a friend in Chester.'

That was miles away. But on my route. I supposed her friend was a she.

'What are you doing here?'

'I work at The Manor Lodge. I'm a receptionist. Front desk. Just done the morning shift. All checking out at once. It's been a difficult day. I'll spare you the details. Just winding down here.'

They're usually good-looking, receptionists. Well made up. Must be, I suppose. And she was no exception. But they're never very receptive to a chat-up I find. Not while working, anyway. But she wasn't on duty then!

'I see a lot of hotels. With my job. I'm a salesman.'

'You see the world then.'

'Such as it is. Ready for another?'

She nodded.

'Same again?'

'Thanks.'

I had to tap the bar with my lighter to get the attention of the barman who was serving in the other bar.

'Same again here. Twice.'

The conversation skipped along easily enough, and I told her the stories I had told many times before. Salesman's tales. Long on interest, short on truth. But they passed the time. And she was hanging on every word as though she'd not heard spiel like it before. But she had, I knew. You don't work in a hotel without hearing a lot of bollocks. And she knew what was coming up. And she knew how she was going to handle it.

'Time please,' announced the barman, cutting in to the conversation.

'Thanks for the drink.'

'It's a pleasure. I hope you're not driving back.'

'No. I've got a little terraced house just off Leaden Hill Road. It's not far.'

'Shall I see you safely home?'

'That'll be nice. Thank you.' She squatted to pick up her handbag from beneath her stool, and I could see her full breasts bulge together above the line of her bra as her blouse fell forwards. Her legs were towards me with one knee slightly above the other, showing a channel of smooth, stockinged thigh and a flash of white underwear. She smiled as she stood up, steadying herself on the rail of the bar. She walked in front of me through the door into the street. I didn't look back. I guessed the barman would be looking at us, and I didn't want to catch his eye.

As we walked, I talked about the village and my mates. 'I met one of them again last night, in The Anchor there. He's a regular. Name of Howard Watson.'

'I know Howard. Usually sits in the corner near the door.'

Knew Howard! Had he given her one then? No. Not Howard. Of all people. Still, he's got some money, and money talks. Probably a flashy car. He might have pulled.

'Yeah, that's him.'

'He comes into The Manor every Sunday lunch with his mother. Started when his father died a few years back now. It was since I started.'

Not Howard, then.

'Do you want to come in for a coffee?'

We'd arrived at the cottage the middle of three down

a side lane. The roadway wasn't made up, and there was no pavement. I remembered it went down to a style and then became a footpath to a small wood. We used to go down there looking for rabbits. We didn't catch any, but the chase was everything. I looked around. I didn't know anybody around here. When I was a lad, the cottages were occupied by old ladies. They'd be gone then. I wasn't going to be recognised here. But Auntie Pauline's was just round the corner. We'd have passed it if we hadn't have turned down here.

'Yeah. OK.' As she turned to put her key in the lock, I tried to look nonchalant. She was on the raised doorstep, and as she reached for the lock, her skirt rode slightly up her leg.

'Come in. Stick your coat over a chair.' She went through to the back and I heard a kettle being filled. I looked around the room. There were a few photographs, several of her and a man, the same one in a wedding photo behind. I walked to the connecting door, and we met in the frame, she pushing herself against me. There was no mistake. I cupped her face in my hands and kissed her long and slow. She gasped slightly, for pleasure or performance I couldn't tell. It made no difference. She put her hands on my buttocks and pulled me to her.

'The coffee will wait. Come on.' She took my hand and towed me up the stairs leading off the front room.

I know I brag a lot about my conquests out on the road, but they're not as often as I pretend or I'd like. But this was a bit different. I was surprised how easily I was sucked into this encounter. Each sip of beer, each embroidered story drew me down this path, and I did not resist. I was easily led, and she was leading me now.

She took me into a room at the back. The curtains were drawn. She kissed me this time, and I could feel her breasts against my chest. She started to unbutton my shirt, and I reached for her blouse buttons. She paused to undo her own cuff buttons and thrust her body forwards to shake off the blouse. Her body was full, with a slight plumpness that made her comfortably inviting. I reached behind to undo her bra. The straps had left a groove in her shoulders. Turning away, she shed her skirt and tights and got under the duvet.

'Come on.'

She was ready straight away. She pulled me onto her, giving me little choice. Not that I wanted any. It was good. Oh my God, it was good. She made it so easy for me. She made no noise, and when I had come, she held me in her, gasping as she came again. I rolled off her, looking for a towel or some tissues. Nothing. She lay there, her eyes shut but not asleep. I looked round the room. Two suitcases were piled on the wardrobe. A cheap mirror hung on the chimney breast, reflecting the wall somewhere above my head. She started to snore.

I looked for my trousers to get a ciggie. They were on the end of the bed. I got up and went on to her bathroom and washed myself. I dressed, and whilst I was fastening my shirt, I stood near the edge of the window looking out between the curtains. There was Auntie Pauline's garden stretching at right angles to the line of this house. The hedges had grown carelessly, and the nearest was a line of leylandii which hid the garden I once knew so well. There would be the simple rectangular lawn with a circular flower bed. The lawn was edged with shrubs – lavender, peonies, hydrangea. And at the bottom of the garden, a compost heap hidden away behind a shield of bushes; they had orange flowers in the early spring, but I didn't know the name. It would be like that because Dad had kept it like that. Just as Auntie Pauline wanted it. Just as it was when Uncle Harry went to war, leaving his wife to share the house with his parents. Until I was old enough to play on my own, I had come with Dad every Sunday morning, and I had helped him dump the grass on the compost heap, weed the flower beds, carry the clippings from the privet hedges. And in the middle of the morning, Auntie Pauline made us a cup of tea and offered us cakes she had made that day. Looking back, it had an innocence which now seemed beautiful. Did I ever look up at the window I was standing at now? And for the thirty-plus years since, Dad had come every Sunday to tend the garden of his dead pal. And that had a beauty too. But he hadn't come recently as the high hedges declared. I supposed Auntie Pauline was in the house at that moment. She seemed always to be there.

I turned back to the bed. She was still asleep. I didn't even know her name. I closed the door quietly and went downstairs and let myself out. Mam was going out and I had to hurry home. Time flies when you're having fun!

'Hello, Peter. You're late. Where've you been?'

There was no time to think carefully. 'I went for a walk. Just to get some fresh air and a change of scene.'

I'd just lied to Mam. Of course, I lied. What's the

point in telling the truth? Am I really going to say I met a strange woman in a pub, we went back to her place and had sex? I might say that to my mates. Even if it wasn't true. But not to Mam. I don't think mothers want to know. But she must have had sex. What did she make of it, up there in that old, heavy bed?

★★★

After my mother went to her church, I ran a bath. The cistern hissed for a long time as it refilled. I had just settled into it when I heard a noise. Was it Dad? I couldn't hear anything. Maybe it was just the water tank. They say there's a death rattle. I wondered what it sounded like. Perhaps he'd died, that minute. On his own. With me only a few feet away. Shit.

I struggled out of the deep-sided bath and pulled a towel around me. I went stealthily to the front bedroom, leaving a trail of wet footprints. I listened. There was silence. I edged in, holding the towel with one hand.

'Dad?' I whispered.

There was no response. I leaned over him and felt his warm breath smelling sourly as it brushed my face. He burped softly and a little bubble of spit ballooned in the corner of his mouth. He was still with us, the old bugger. I was so pleased.

I returned to the bathroom, pausing to rest my forehead for a moment on its door jamb. I was close to tears. I really was. I left the bathroom door open and got back in the bath. The water was cool, but I didn't want to run any more. I had to listen out for Dad.

I was looking after Dad then, just like he used to look after me, when I was ill. And when I had those nightmares after Billy died. Jesus, I was frightened then. But he came quickly when I woke. And now I'm listening out for him. But I couldn't ease his nightmare, could I? Poor him. Poor me.

I washed myself as quietly as I could, giving my old man a really good soaping. I hoped I'd not caught something. It took enough explaining the last time. Maureen's never been the same since. Always insisted on a johnny. What a turn-off. None of this trouble for Dad, eh. Although I don't know. What about the war? Away from home for months on end. He must have… well, you know. It's only natural, isn't it. He didn't talk about it when we sat with our cigs at the end of the garden, did he? Well, he wouldn't, would he? And neither would I. Not to my son anyway. William. Christ. I wonder, has he been up to it? Bloody youngsters these days. You can't trust them an inch.

I sat downstairs in my pyjamas and dressing gown until my mother came in. She wasn't late, but I didn't want to stay up with her.

'How's Dad?'

'No change. He didn't make a sound.' It was like he was already dead.

'Good.'

'Did you have a good time, Mam?'

I didn't mean a *good time*, Mam, I meant a nice time.

'Yes. It was a real treat. There was a good turnout. Special guest, you see. You've no idea what they have to put up with in Africa.'

I'm sure she was right, but I didn't have a clue.

'I think I'll get an early night. See you in the morning.'

'Thanks, Peter. You're a good lad.'

Is that what Mam thought? A good lad. That's something.

'Goodnight.'

'Goodnight.'

WEDNESDAY

On the third morning I went for a walk around the village to see what had changed, hoping little had. I had no doubt as to which way I should go, and I turned right at the gate. Away from The Anchor, away from Auntie Pauline's, away from… temptation? I hoped I wouldn't meet anybody who would recognise me in case I didn't recognise them, and they thought me rude. At the same time, I wanted to be noticed; if Eldon blotted me out, who would claim me? I was heading for the church and the bridge crossing the river.

Before long I passed a housing estate on the other side of the road overlooking the playing fields which had given so much freedom all those years ago. It stretched back into the fields and curved round the back of the church. I couldn't tell how big it was. It had one entry road called St. George's Way – after the church, I supposed. It was another example of the village being stretched into some future world, pulling on the bands that had kept the place together in my childhood. I stood looking up the entrance road and I decided, without any evidence, that no one on the estate would know who I was; just rural yuppies. I doubted they attended events at the community hall or crossed the threshold of the Legion.

But these were sour thoughts. I thought when I came back it was just to see my father die, but the longer I was here, the more I was being dragged back into the world I thought I had escaped.

Further on, was what I had thought of as the centre of the village. Across the road was The Church Inn, then the church itself with its crowded graveyard, and a war memorial between them, the last of these soon to be surrounded by old soldiers, young widows and curious toddlers on Remembrance Sunday.

On my side of the road was an open square bordered by a rectangle of shops. The shops were on a slightly higher level than the square to allow for flooding from the river beyond. This created a surrounding platform from which generations of toddlers could jump with safety to the square below. It was unfenced in my day but now it was railed off, health and safety trumping adventure. On the far edge of the square stood buildings, still familiar. There was the police station where Sergeant Pinnock loomed large. There were the council offices combined with the library to which our teachers had directed us to read the classics, the atlases, the encyclopaedias, the history of England, but where we rarely got beyond Biggles and W.E. Johns, the people of the world no more real than the cunning Orientals and moustachioed South Americans of post-war children's comics. There we sampled *Just William*, imagining ourselves as his gang and jealous of their disregard for the bidding of adults but, even at that young age feeling that their lives, their homes, their parents were something detached from ours, a different class I recognise now. There was the post office inside a little shop selling tobacco, newspapers and sweets which were an easy target for young boys sampling crime despite Sergeant Pinnock next door.

On the road edge of the square stood two buildings like sentinels either side of the entrance to the shopping area beyond – the community hall and the British Legion clubhouse. Dad had much to do with both of them – helping to build the first and keeping the other alive.

In the middle of the square was a tree, mature now, though I don't remember it. It was surrounded by some wooden benches which enjoyed its shade. On one of them sat, next to each other, two elderly men, dressed for the autumn weather – one wore a trilby, the other a flat cap. Both were protected by substantial overcoats. I imagined them recalling lives past, but they could just as easily be talking about the weather, the football results, last night's TV or the price of cigarettes, without recalling the familiar stories of their earlier lives. One had a dog tethered to an arm of the bench. It lay flat on the ground, its front paws supporting its head as it watched the world go by. Do dogs have memories? Of course they do, but how much and for how long?

A young woman crossed the square pushing a child's buggy. The two men greeted the pair, and the dog raised itself, stretched its lead to maximum and sniffed at the pushchair. The infant shrieked. What would this infant remember, I wondered? There must be an age when memories can take root, leaving the desert of infancy behind; then the present can begin to create a past.

I crossed the road to the church gate. The posters on the church noticeboard confirmed Mr Baverstock as the vicar and listed the many community events that were to take place nearby – Mam's social among them. I didn't want to go into the graveyard; I knew Billy was there, and I didn't want to confront that now.

And then the river, running at right angles to the road, as though shielding the green fields beyond from development. It had a name, but I'd forgotten it. We called it "The River", though now it seemed little more than a stream, rejuvenated after summer's warmth by last week's autumn rain. We played in it. Of course, we did. What are streams for? In the summer months when the level was low, we could wade in it without it overlapping our wellies – and even if it did flood them, what's the big deal with wet socks? Here we trapped tiddlers in jam jars, tried to catch elusive eels with home-made hooks, grouped stones together in a forlorn attempt to dam the flow, bent low beneath the arch of the bridge, shouting to cause ricocheting echoes. In the winter, we hoped for frosts severe enough to freeze the river over so that we might skate on it. But it was never quite hard enough and, fortunately for us perhaps, we had to be content with breaking up the frozen fringes of the water with branches we found on the ground below the trees lining the banks. All this we must have done in a few short years between infancy and puberty, before other currents tugged at our bodies.

The other side of the river had a fence a few yards

back with an all-weather path between it and the water. This was new, to me at least. Two solid armed benches stood against the fence, and I went down to sit on one. It had a rectangular brass plaque which read: *In memory of Robert Pritchard who looked from here over the community he called home.*

It was a familiar name, and then I remembered. Of course. Mr Pritchard, the headmaster of our primary school. Did he spend all his life here in Eldon? Happy? Content? Not restless like me. But what did my restlessness bring me more than the serenity of Eldon brought him? Not much, I thought.

I speculated on what had held Mr Pritchard's attention. Certainly, the church had the chocolate-box appeal of most churches, and many of his friends would have been in the graveyard – him as well, I expect. Did he believe in the whole religious thing? We sang hymns at school, but doesn't that go with the job? Was he looking back on his life or looking forward to an eternal life? If he sat here after the housing estate was built, surely he could not have cherished that view. The houses now blotted out much of the land beyond, but there, between two of the houses, I could see the roof of the primary school perched on the edge of Leaden Hill Road. In his day, he would have seen much more of the school, perhaps could have heard the voices of youngsters playing at break times, seen the Union Jack hoisted on special occasions. All that gone now, hidden by development. How many of the village's children had passed through his care? How many did he remember? Did he remember *me*? If he didn't, who *would* have remembered me? I wanted to be remembered.

I didn't want my life to be chipped away by every death in the village. Bits of me going into each open grave until there was nothing left of me in Eldon. When I lived here, I wanted to be free of it, but now I was free, I needed a safe haven to be anchored to.

An elderly woman came through the church gate carrying a bunch of flowers. She located the grave she wanted with no uncertainty and removed some dead flowers from a vase, replacing them with her new ones. Walking to a corner of the graveyard, she threw the dead flowers on a compost heap. She had brought a large bottle with her, and this she filled from a tap alongside the heap. On returning to the grave, she filled the vase and put the bottle in her bag. Moving to the end of the grave, she faced the etched headstone and stood still for a minute or so, her head not bowed but upright as she faced the chiselled inscription. Someone was remembering, and someone was being celebrated. A lifetime – two lifetimes – were passing through her mind.

I found her presence lightened my mood. It was so easy to see these hundreds of graves as sucking life out of the world like a giant sieve, leaving sadness where there had been happiness. But there was another way of seeing them: they took the sorrow with them, leaving behind more positive things. What does religion say about all this?

She stood still for a moment, not apparently praying, before leaving the graveyard the way she had come. Was she warm inside, leaving the cold in the graveyard? I hoped so.

For a moment, I imagined it to be Mam, for surely at some point in the future she would be doing this in memory of a life past – hers and Dad's. But I'd stopped looking into the past; now I was looking at the future – Dad's – and hers... and mine. Something cold went through me. Those stories of treading on your future grave became reality.

But that was daft. Sitting on a bench alongside a river in autumn weather is bound to make you cold. And anyway, my grave wasn't going to be down there; I'd got away; I'd escaped. Hadn't I?

I sat for a while, the village just far enough away for its clamour to be masked by the sound of the river that was indifferent to the people whose lives it passed through. Those banks cleaned with every flood would not remember me, though I remembered them. I looked up and down the banks, hoping I would recognise a tree or a bend in the river. But it was all new; nature doesn't stand still. Does nature have memory?

Nothing could be heard from the school, but I knew what was under that roof – the little hall, the half a dozen classrooms, the toilets tiled in a sickly green. I could see it now, lodged in my brain with all those other memories of this community waiting to be released by... what?

As he sat here – how long ago? – Mr Pritchard had seen his school – my school too – and had remembered and been content. Mr Pritchard, I remember you. Did you remember me?

★★★

After lunch I pushed open the door to The Anchor and went through to the bar.

'Howard! Fancy seeing you here!'

'There's no need to be sarcastic, Peter. I admit I spend a lot of time here. It's a second home. You try living with your mother. What'll you have?'

'A pint of that.' The barman shifted his hand from one pump to another.

'Wednesday is market day at Fincham, and I usually pop in for a drink on the way home – give it a miss in the evening.'

'I spent quite a bit of time in here with Gordon. Gary and Bendy went somewhere else.'

'You lot were always a bit rough on me, you know. You were cruel at times.'

'Yeah. I suppose we were. You put up with it though.'

'Well, you were my heroes, in a way.'

'Heroes? Christ!'

'Well, you seemed not to care about things. You could do silly, dangerous things. Exactly the things my parents told me not to do.'

'But you did them, anyway.'

'Well, I suppose we all rebel against something. I wanted to rebel against conformity, but I didn't have the courage to do it on my own. I can see that now.'

'You've worked things out, haven't you?'

'Well, I spend a lot of my time in this bar, thinking—'

'And drinking,' I interrupted.

'Yes, and drinking. But not just here. You'd be surprised how much time you get to think on a farm.'

'I expect that's why so many farmers top themselves. Thinking's dangerous, Howard. I try to avoid it.'

'You were always the one for doing things. Getting up to pranks.'

'And Gordon. He used to egg me on.'

'If that's what you like to think.'

'Well, what's all this thinking done for you? You're still here, in the same village, in the same house. Where's it got you?'

'Nowhere really. I still don't have the courage to branch out.'

'But you've got the money. You could do almost anything you want.'

'I suppose I don't have the hunger for anything. You always wanted to get on.'

'Well get out first. Then get on. I could see myself just stagnating here. Just like Dad.'

'Just like me.'

'But you had the choice. I had no money, no qualifications, no prospects. I either went or I sank.'

'And has it come good?'

'Yeah. Yeah, it has in a way. I've got a good job. People look up to me, people in the company, I mean.'

'So, you're happy?'

'No, I don't think so. If I was happy, I wouldn't be restless. And if I wasn't restless, I wouldn't get on. It's as simple as that. Mam and Dad were happy. Well, they seemed to be. They've lived here since they were married. What, fifty years near enough. But they're poor. That wasn't enough for me. Don't get me wrong. I loved it as a kid here. With my parents. With you and the gang. School was OK. But once I joined the army, I knew it wasn't enough. I knew it could be better.'

'But, in fact, you were *taken* away, weren't you? By

the army, I mean. Would you have gone if it wasn't for national service?'

'I'll never know that. I like to think so. But it doesn't matter. It happened. I got away.'

'And you don't want to come back?'

'No way. I'm glad it's here, mind. It's comforting to come back here.'

'Why, when you wanted to get away?'

'It's so simple here, I suppose. So uncomplicated. So protective.'

'Yes. I agree. And that's what I like. I think it's why I'm content to stay.'

'How come you didn't do national service then, Howard? You're older than me; you should have gone. Did you drop them a back-hander or something?'

'Certainly not. I was medically unfit.'

'Knock-kneed you mean.'

'Now, now.'

'Well, what, then?'

'Not something I'm going to tell you about. You'd just take the piss.'

'I expect you're right. It didn't suit everybody. Some poor sod topped himself in our hut. Not in the hut, I mean, but outside the camp. He—'

Howard interrupted, 'I'd rather not know, thank you. Death's not a good subject for conversation.'

'No.'

'Anyway, changing the subject, I've got some news. I've been in touch with Bendy and Gary, and they can be free on Saturday. We're going up to The Farmers Arms at Fincham for a meal. Just the four of us. Like the old days.'

'No Gordon?'

'No. No one knows where he is. If you can find him, I'll invite him.'

'What about Directory Enquiries?'

'With a name like Smith? No chance.'

'I see what you mean.'

'The Farmers has changed as you'll see. We used to go up there when I first had a car. Before you were old enough to go in pubs. They've done it up. It's a bit trendy, but we're going for old times' sake, not the decor. I'll pick you up at your mother's at about seven. Bendy and Gary are going up separately. By the way, don't talk to Bendy about his wife. There's something going on. I don't know what.'

'And Gary?'

'Happily married. No problems.'

'So, just like the old days then.' Except for Gordon… and Billy.

'I understand you met Sally Ryan yesterday.'

'Who?'

'The receptionist from The Manor.'

Christ. I never even asked her name. But she didn't ask mine either. 'Right. Yeah, she was here when I popped in yesterday lunchtime.'

'Good-looking woman.'

'Perhaps she's looking for a rich husband. You could land on your feet there, Howard – or on your back.'

'I don't think so. She's already married. So they tell me at The Manor. Mother's quite friendly with the couple who own it. Her husband's away somewhere. Some talk of prison, I understand.'

I didn't want this conversation going on. I didn't know where it would end. I emptied the glass, and although I could have done with another, I had to get away.

'Well, I've got to get on, Howard. I promised Mam I wouldn't be out long. Mothers, eh.'

'Yes. Quite. See you on Saturday, Peter.'

THURSDAY

The next morning, in what was becoming a routine, I gave Dad his breakfast. I slowly spooned in the creamy porridge. He couldn't take mouthfuls without squeezing some out over the edge of the spoon. It fell on the tea towel covering the bedclothes. It was like feeding the kids again. I was glad to do it, though I knew I wasn't building up a growing body. Just keeping going an ancient wreck – like his bike. I could feel his gums pressing on the edges of the spoon and wondered if it hurt. He would be too frail to complain. He wouldn't have complained even if he could speak. Not him. Dad.

'Come on now, just one more mouthful. Open your mouth and let the train in the tunnel.' I was glad to be doing something for him. Even though it was too late. 'Had enough? OK. Have a drink then.'

I looked around the room. Everything seemed drab, faded. Is that what happens when people live in a place for a long time? Their surroundings become tired and colourless just as they do themselves. And familiarity and habit stop them seeing the slow downward change.

Maureen would have made changes every few years, redecorated the walls, replaced the curtains, taken down the pictures; she doesn't do pictures, doesn't Maureen. I'm glad she does it, as it stops me from fading too.

Afterwards, while Mam was helping the nurse to wash Dad, I went to the bottom of the garden and sat on the bench we'd sat on together so often. It was tucked away behind some mature shrubs. In those days, it had been a sort of secret hideaway, somewhere where the men could be alone. I hadn't noticed how peaceful and quiet it was. But at that time, I was not looking for peace and quiet. I was now.

I lit a cigarette and it helped. I leant forwards, my elbows on my knees, my head facing downwards. I didn't like this. Either I wanted Dad back, fit and well, reliable, comforting, or I wanted him gone. His dying was dirty. I wanted to wash his death off me. But I couldn't do anything about it.

I reached forward and pulled at one of the weeds in the flower bed. It came easily from the well-tilled autumn soil. Its roots hung down pathetically, no longer able to give life to their parent plant. It wouldn't live again, this tiny plant, and it didn't matter. I threw it to the ground. I flicked the cigarette butt into the shrubs and decided to go to the pub after lunch, not knowing what to expect.

★★★

She wasn't there, so I just had the one pint and left. When I got to the main road, I turned left and then right up Leaden Hill Road. I knew it took me past her road and had a faint hope she might be around, not that I would have knocked at her door. And what was I expecting anyway? It took me past Auntie Pauline's as well, but I wasn't going to call there either, for reasons I couldn't fathom; I always felt awkward with her – she always looked at me oddly.

But just opposite was the primary school where I had spent half a childhood before going off to the secondary modern school in Wellworth. Outwardly, it seemed just the same: a playground at the front and sides, from which boys and girls separated until they went into their own entrances when the bell went. Yet in class we sat together – well, opposite halves of the room – what was that all about? But it changed one year, didn't it? When we went into Juniors and Mr Pritchard replaced Miss Garrett. There were still separate toilets, and we used to take bets to see who would run into the girls' toilets – not money but conkers or playing cards. I nearly got a complete set of Turf cards once. I don't know the theme; was it footballers or film stars? It didn't seem to matter; collecting was the point. The playground was empty. I assumed all the kids were inside studying, studying what? What did I learn?

The capital of France is Paris.
Twelve twelves are one hundred and forty-four.
Complete the saying: "As brown as a…"
There are sixteen ounces in a pound and twenty shillings in a pound. Not the same pound.
Saint George is the patron saint of England.
The national anthem – first verse only.

The ten commandments. All of them.

If it didn't make sense, it didn't have to. It's what we learnt. We didn't learn to argue, to disagree, to discover, to protest; these things I learnt later. But here you took it in, or you failed. Your mind couldn't wander; the bottom of the windows was well above our height, so the only thing to see outside was the sky.

One memory was firmly fixed. At break times, perhaps when I was climbing the front railings of the playground, or taking a break from some game to lean my back against the knobbly stone wall, or sitting on the empty crates that had brought the morning milk, I would glance at Auntie Pauline's and, more often than not, I could see her face at an upstairs window. If not a face, then a moving curtain. She was not there when Mam met me after school, but as I got older and could come home without her – with Gordon of course – I'm sure Auntie Pauline was watching me walking down the hill until hidden by the tree on the corner of the playing fields where Leaden Hill Road met the main Wellworth Road. It was good for climbing that tree was.

All these scenes played out in my mind when I heard a vehicle pull up behind me; it was a police car with a single bobby in it. He came alongside me.

'Good afternoon, sir. Waiting for someone?'

I could see that *What's it got to do with you?* would not have been a good response. I tried to explain my motives, but they looked suspicious. Isn't it always the case that when you talk to a copper you feel guilty and probably look guilty as well?

'Is there a problem?'

He gave me a lecture involving problems with lone men lurking around schools. I had some sympathy, what with that incident with Claire. He asked me where I was staying, and I told him the address.

'Isn't that Eric Carter's house?'

I nodded. 'You know him then?'

'No. I don't know him personally, but he and my dad are in a little group who play cards at the Legion. How is he?'

I explained, and after he suggested hanging about a school wasn't a good idea for a man of my age – not these days – he returned to his car and drove off.

My age! The cheeky bastard.

It was all so trivial, yet it had soured my return to a place I had considered simple and innocent. Yet here, it was being dragged into the sullied world of the big town. I turned to go back home and felt sure I saw a curtain twitch in Auntie Pauline's house.

FRIDAY

She was there the next day after lunch, sitting in the corner where Howard usually sat. I saw her as soon as I got in, because I was looking for her, I suppose.

'Hi.' She got her greeting in first.

I asked did she want a drink, but she put her hand over her glass and shook her head. I ordered a pint at the bar and joined her, sitting on a stool with my back to the bar to avoid any earwigging by the barman. I didn't know what to say, so I picked up my glass.

'My name's Sally, by the way. Sally Ryan. I don't think we introduced ourselves.'

Well, it was a bit casual.

'I'm Peter, Peter Carter.'

'Yes, I know. Howard told me.'

'What else did he say?'

'Not much. Just stuff about schooldays. He's here quite a lot when I drop in on the way home.'

No more then?

'He needs the company I expect.'

'I'm sorry about the other day,' she said, as I took my first sip.

'For what exactly?'

'Falling asleep.'

'Well, it wasn't exactly the best response I've had. And do you usually chat up the other drinkers?'

'No, but Tuesday was a bad day. One of the guests committed suicide during the night and I had to deal with it until the manager arrived. One of the maids called me in. What do you do? There is this body obviously dead, so no help needed. Where do you look to get information – next of kin and so on. There's a procedure of course, but when things happen, you're still not sure what to do. I found a telephone number in the end and spoke to a woman. What should I say? Was he her husband, or fiancé, or partner, or father, or brother? "I'm so sorry but…" I'd been up since six o'clock, and that early shift can be very hard work if lots of people have to check out. And you have to keep smiling. Can't show what you really feel. So, I was feeling very sorry for myself and needed cheering up.'

'So, you popped into the pub for a shag.'

'I didn't plan it, and there were two of us.'

'But one of us kept awake.'

'I've said I'm sorry. I know what you're thinking.'

'Surprise me.'

'I've been having a difficult time recently, and I needed a bit of easy conversation and a bit of company.'

'And a quickie.'

'It's not just men who fancy uncommitted sex, you know. We may be a bit fussier over who we choose.'

'So why did you choose me?'

I wanted her to say it was my incredibly good looks and irresistible charm, but she didn't.

'If I said there wasn't much choice – four pensioners at the back, a teenager behind the bar and you – you would take offence. However, there was a cockiness about you which suggested you would be game for... you know.'

I wasn't sure about the cockiness, but yes, I thought I was a man of the world.

'There must be more than that. I could have been really bad news for you.'

'Yes. I know. I suppose the risk was part of the attraction. What do they call it? An aphrodisiac. Yes, that's it. I can't deny that. But we talked quite a lot, and it doesn't take long to see what someone's like underneath.'

'Feminine intuition, you mean.'

'If you like.'

'So, what are you after then?'

'Just like I said. I thought I'd treat myself to a bit of nice sex. I thought I deserved it. I'd been without it for... well, never mind.'

She was upfront, I'd give her that.

'What about the consequences?'

'Well, I don't suppose I gave them much thought at the time. You don't when sex is uppermost in your mind.'

'But there can *be* consequences.'

'Well, if you want chapter and verse, I knew I wasn't going to get pregnant. I might have caught something from you, and that was a bit careless.'

'I think you're OK there.'

'Hmm. Pardon me if I'm sceptical. But I also knew you weren't going to be a pain in the arse, wanting to see me again and all that crap.'

'How did you know that?'

'Well, most men are pretty transparent, and I reckon you'd be scared to death if I wanted to follow it up. That's not what you want. You want it now, thank you and goodnight.'

'Well, thanks.'

'Am I right?'

Of course she was right, but I didn't want it spelt out for me. She talked a good talk this lady. And she hadn't run off, had she?

'So, if I asked, "Do you want me to take you home now?" – and all the rest – then you'd say yes.'

'No. I wouldn't.'

'Why not, for Christ's sake?'

That was a mistake. She knew she'd rattled me now.

'Because I'm not feeling now what I was feeling the other day.'

'Maybe that's because I did you a bit of good. Perhaps you need some more.' I liked that line.

'You don't understand women, do you? I'm sure you've known a lot. In bed, I mean. But you don't understand them.'

She was right on both counts. I just hoped she just didn't ask: how many? I could kid myself there had been a lot. A bit of fumbling doesn't count.

'What's there to understand?'

I should not have asked that.

'It would take too long. And we don't have the time.'

'But look, you've sat here all this time chatting with me, yet you don't want to go to bed with me. I don't get it.'

'That's what I mean. I've enjoyed sitting here talking. Really enjoyed it. You've been good company. But I don't need all that grunting and sweating. Not at this moment.'

I'd never heard a woman talk like this before. I didn't know what to make of her. I wasn't going to get my end away, that's for sure.

She gathered up her handbag and small umbrella and made to go. She paused and looked straight at me. 'What are you doing on Sunday evening?'

Well, as things stood, I would be watching *Songs of Praise* with Mam.

'I've no plans.'

'It's my day off. I'd like to cook you a meal. I haven't done that in ages.'

'Is that all that's on offer?'

She smiled. 'Who knows. Just come. Around seven. Don't bring anything, and don't expect anything. OK?'

'OK.'

★★★

I went home and gave Dad his tea. I didn't mind feeding him by then. At first, I was frightened, but then I sort of enjoyed it. Sitting on the bed close to him. Chatting. He must have heard what I was saying. He was eating, so he was conscious, wasn't he? I talked about all the things he'd made me in his shed. How I used to take the little models to school to show my mates. Where were those models now? Not thrown away, surely. I'd left them here when I went away. Left them with all the other things I wanted to leave behind. I suppose I wanted to leave Dad too.

I didn't talk about the things I'd left for. The cars, the money, the holidays, the house, the bit on the side, the bits on the side. I didn't want to talk of those things. I didn't want Dad to hear. He didn't want to hear, did he? I could have told him what I did the other afternoon after the pub shut. But I wouldn't. I didn't want him to hear. I didn't want him to hear that I was going to lie to Mam when I'd finished here.

I told him about my night out the next day with Howard and the rest. I told him about Howard's farm and Gary's business. But I didn't tell him about the other things. There must have been something wrong if I didn't want to tell him. I checked the radiator was working and left him with the bedroom door slightly ajar so we could hear if he called. I tiptoed down the stairs. I had to hold the banister to avoid tumbling down. In the end I went sideways. Why is it easier to go up stairs than down?

'Is it all right if I leave you alone on Sunday evening? I thought I'd go down to the pub. Howard and I might go off for a meal.'

'Yes. That's fine with me. You are in during the day, so I can go to church, aren't you? I'd like to go in the afternoon as well. To Sunday school. Just to hear the little ones singing.'

'No, that's OK. I'll man the ship.' It made me feel a lot better about going out that evening.

'I thought you were going out with Howard *tomorrow*.'

'Well, yes, but we thought we might go out on Sunday as well. Just the two of us. With it being the weekend. Howard needs a bit of company.'

'Good idea. Where will you go do you think?'

I was about to lie to Mam. I'd lied a few times in my life but didn't want to lie to *her*.

'I don't know. Howard knows the places to go. He'll find somewhere nice.' I'd lied.

SATURDAY

I thought I'd bring the telly up into Dad's room so he could watch something about gardening of home improvements, but there was no aerial point in the room. Can you believe that? Only one TV socket in the whole house.

I looked round for a portable radio. Nothing. There was the old set in his shed, the one we had inside for years. It was powered by a wet acid battery which I used to carry to the shed and exchange for another that had been charging all week it seemed. That was my special grown-up job. Mam used to warn me about spilling the acid on myself. And even when Mam insisted on a mains radio for the house, he still kept the old one in the shed. He'd charge the batteries up from the power point on the same bench. He wouldn't throw it away; said it received more stations than the modern ones. And I used to turn the dials, picking up whistles and shrieks from all over Europe, all over the world, he said. And he might have been right. A lot of history had come out of that set, he said. He'd heard about the Korean War, the death of the king when all the home radio programmes were taken off the air and there were only the overseas ones to listen to, the coronation, the ascent of Everest. He never was one for sport, so he didn't bother with Cup finals and Grand Nationals.

And Sunday mornings was when he went to do Auntie Pauline's garden, every Sunday morning, regular as clockwork. I used to go with him for a while. Auntie Pauline would get me some biscuits and some pop when I got tired of helping Dad. She showed me pictures of Dad and her husband, Harry, in their uniforms. Uncle Harry – I don't have an image of him – was killed right next to Dad. 'Just there,' he said that day on the hidden bench and pointed to the lilac bush. So, Auntie Pauline had no one to do the garden, and Dad did it. Good old Dad.

I thought I should pop in and see Auntie Pauline. I hadn't seen her for years. She never came to us. Hardly left the house it seemed. Still, I should visit her just for Dad's sake. Why didn't I want to? I hoped she didn't want any gardening doing; cutting Dad's hedge was enough for me.

I thought I could ask him about Auntie Pauline, but he'd nodded off again.

'I'll see you later.'

I got up to leave the room but paused at the door. I looked back at him. If I didn't say things now, it would be too late. No good talking to a coffin. But he was asleep.

I'd been a bit of a shit in my life if the truth were known. Cheated on Maureen. Fiddled my expenses. And he wasn't like that. He was a man I could admire, could look up to. And he made me look cheap… I begged him not to leave me.

★★★

Howard arrived spot on seven. Typical! I was waiting in the front room so saw his Rover pull up. Mam came behind me to the gate. Howard wound down the driver's window.

'Hello, Howard. How's your mother?'

I hoped Mam wouldn't mention Sunday night.

'She's OK, Mrs Carter.'

'Remember me to her.'

'I will.'

'And, Howard,' I feared what might come next, 'tell her there's a bring-and-buy at the church on Thursday afternoon. Ask if she can spare anything for it. It's in aid of Africa.'

'See you later, Mam. Now go in out of the cold. Don't wait up.'

It was probably more than twenty years since I had last taken that trip, and any sense of familiarity was deadened by the changes in road signs and hedgerows in that time. The pub, too, had lost any claim on my youth. Then, it had been a simple country pub, almost indifferent to casual trade, its decor reflecting an earlier age. Now, its new owners had struck a more strident tone. It advertised itself to the world as a pub restaurant by the large sign near the corner of the minor road on which it stood and the main road along which we came.

Howard and I stood for a few moments with our

backs to the car, looking at the pub. On the frontage were several picnic tables, unoccupied in the autumn gloom. They were covered by a coating of rain from the light shower that had just passed through, and the lights from inside the pub reflected off the wet surfaces.

'Do you remember the first time we came here?'

'No, it's a bit of a blur. We came here quite a lot when you got your car.'

'It was Bendy's birthday. His eighteenth. Don't you remember?'

That was over twenty-five years ago.

'You've got a good memory.'

'I was the only one who was sober. I had to stop for Gary and Bendy to be sick. I think you and Gordon were a bit more used to the beer than them.'

We knew how to hold it even then. Even before we used to go off together down to The George in Cooksley.

'Are you looking forward to seeing the others?'

I wasn't really. We were not going to have much in common. And they'd been stuck here all their lives.

'Sure am, Howard. Just like old times, eh!'

The pub was not as I recalled, but I'd seen a lot of pubs since then. I got out and waited while Howard locked up. He'd got a personalised number plate. Posy bastard. I didn't really mean that. I'd tried to get one once. Nearest I could find was PWC a hundred and something. I didn't want the W anyway.

Howard saw me looking at it.

'I know. I know. But my parents got it for my fortieth. There it was, motor and all, inside the big barn. They'd had it delivered when I was out. I couldn't say no.'

I wouldn't have said no, mate, either. I don't say no to many things.

I followed Howard inside, and there they were, just round the corner of the door. I didn't know what to think. They looked self-conscious too. Gary got up, and Bendy followed him a moment later. We all shook hands. We wouldn't have done that before. It showed what different people we had become. Not just different from then but different from each other. Gary wore a neat shirt and tie underneath a linen jacket. Bendy had a denim top over a T-shirt with some writing on it. I couldn't read what it said, but there was a beer mug just above it. I suppose we called him Bendy because his name was Benedict. Whenever the teacher read out his name from the register, we would whisper "Bendy" and smile schoolboy grins. Benedict!

Gary spoke first. 'Hello, Peter. We meet again. You've done well by the look of you. How are you?'

Overweight he meant, the cheeky bastard, and him looking so trim.

'I'm OK, mate. And yourself? Hiya, Bendy.'

Bendy was looking a bit rough. That long hair didn't suit him. Not cut like that anyway.

Bendy nodded. 'We've been put here to study the menu. She'll be back for the orders later.'

'Are you ready for another?' I looked at their drinks, which they'd hardly touched. Both declined. 'Howard?'

'A mineral water for me, please. I've got to get you home safe, or your mother will never forgive me.'

'Mineral water! This is meant to be a reunion.'

'Of grown-ups, not lads. Not anymore,' grunted Bendy. He was going to be a bundle of fun.

'I don't drink a lot now. I've got my license to think of too,' said Gary.

'You look as though you look after yourself.'

'Well, I'm up and down ladders all the time. Painting and decorating.'

'Yeah, Howard said.'

'And I do a bit of running. I did a half marathon last year.'

Jogging. Fucking hell. I'd rather die.

We sat around and talked about what we were doing now. Not a lot of detail. We talked about Dad, but not about Bendy's wife. We talked about the old days, and although we all shared the same stories, I don't suppose any of us saw them the same way now. It didn't matter. It was a revisiting of a time we all enjoyed. It was carefree in a way my life had failed to be since, and even our bad behaviour was threaded through with innocence. I can't deny that although I detested the kind of life Eldon had promised, there was a simplicity about it which I now missed.

We made our choices from the menu, and Howard ordered some wine for the table, on him, he said, and we didn't argue. We always knew Howard had more money than us and didn't mind spending it on us. I suppose we took advantage, but he was happy to do it, and it all seemed so natural. I suppose we all gave and took from the group, but it never seemed important what it was or how we did it. We understood we were a group that shared something that made us one. We could never escape it, and we could never talk about it. We had another round, but only Bendy and me had pints. Howard told the waitress to put it on the bill.

We went into the restaurant. Howard and I sat next to each other, and Bendy was next to me. Me and him I shifted most of the wine, and after an aside to the waitress by Howard, another one arrived.

'You don't have to pay for everything. We're not beggars,' said Bendy truculently.

I tried to calm things down. 'Go easy, Bendy. Don't be so ungrateful. Howard's just being friendly. We can settle up afterwards.'

Howard had always been the odd one out. He had more money of course, but that wasn't all of it. We all went to the local primary school. Howard was a year older than us, though we were in the same class. He'd been held back a year with some kind of illness. He didn't describe it, and we never asked. Mr Pritchard would know us all. When it came to the eleven-plus, Howard passed and went to the grammar school in Wellworth, and so did Gordon. Bendy, Gary and me went to the secondary modern. Since both schools were in Wellworth, we all went on the same bus which picked me, Gordon, Bendy and Gary up at the stop beyond my house before turning off up the Wellworth Road. Howard was already on the bus which passed the end of the lane to his farm. In Wellworth, Howard and Gordon got off at the stop for the grammar school, and the other three of us (musketeers, eh) stayed on until it reached the sec mod. When we tumbled out of the bus, the boys and girls separated into two groups, each with its own interests. As we got older, pairs of boys and girls began to emerge, and they sat together on the bus, sneaking a kiss as the bus emptied. Another division emerged that had little to do with sex; the gap between the grammar and sec mod kids on the bus became more pronounced. For Howard, both divisions were unwelcome; he wanted to belong. But surprisingly, after two years, he left the school and went to an independent boarding school in Derbyshire.

'You thought you were one of us, but you went to that posh school to get away from us.' Bendy seemed bent on confrontation.

'For the record, I didn't want to go to that school, but my parents insisted I would get better qualifications and make friendships that would be of benefit to me in later life. Besides, I'd lost a year's schooling already.'

'So, we wouldn't have helped you get on, eh?' Bendy was getting louder.

'Well, would we? What would we have offered?' Gary chipped in.

'I went there for three years until I was seventeen, and then it was decided I should do A levels.'

'Was decided. Decided for you. You had no choice?' I joined the interrogation.

'My parents thought that A levels in English Literature, Economics and History were just what I needed.'

'To run a farm? Come off it.'

'They were more ambitious than that. They hoped I would go on to university. You must remember both my parents came from farming families and, until the quarry came to our rescue, we'd no real money. I think my mother's father couldn't read or write. Wouldn't your families have wanted the same for you?'

'If we'd had the money.' Bendy again.

'Exactly. So don't blame me for being well off.'

'So did you get your A levels then?'

'No. I gave up after a term. It wasn't just that the subjects were pointless, but I didn't like the atmosphere in the school – the staff or the boys.'

'Oh. Tell us more.'

'I heard them say things about ordinary people – people like you if you like – which upset me. Remember I'd shared life with you for a long time. If I belong anywhere, I belong in this little town. I didn't belong in that school.'

'Did you object to what they said?'

'No, I just kept my head down, even when I was picked on. I'll give you an example, although it doesn't tell the whole story. In English, we were studying an author called E.M. Forster. You probably won't know him.'

'What makes you think we wouldn't know him?' I asked, defensively.

'Do you?' retorted Howard.

We all shook our heads.

'At the end of one lesson, the English teacher told the class that next time we would be starting on *Howards End* and we should all study it carefully overnight so that the following day we would get to the bottom of it. There was a lot of sniggering, and I could see the teacher knew what he was saying. I expect he used that joke every year so it might not have been directed at me. Everyone was called by their surname so he might not have known I was called Howard. But the boys knew. Life was very uncomfortable for the next few days. Voices shouting across the quad: "Show us your end, Howard," and "let's get to the bottom of this," and all that kind of stuff.'

I thought that quite funny, but it wasn't me on the end of it. Bendy was laughing heartily.

But I knew what Howard meant about your parents wanting the best for you and being prepared to pay for it if they could. I began to think about them, and what with Howard's tale and several pints of bitter, I was getting maudlin about my parents.

'My parents always wanted the best for me. I've never heard a cross word between Mam and Dad. Never. And Dad always had time for me, making me things, showing me things. Always seemed content with life. I envy him.'

'Still found time to visit his lady friend though,' said Bendy, slurring his words rather.

I looked at him but didn't understand what he meant. There was a pause in the conversation, each not wanting to say more.

'Lady friend?'

'That widow on Leaden Hill Road, opposite the school.'

'Auntie Pauline? He used to do her garden for her. That's all.'

'That's all! That's not what they say.'

My mind was haywire. I needn't to think clearly. I understood what Bendy meant, but it didn't make sense. Beer and wine don't mix at the best of times. But they were not the only things to cause confusion.

'Who says? Says what?'

'That he was screwing her. While your mother was

at church, he was getting his end away with the lady on Leaden Hill Road.'

I couldn't stop it. My mind was out of control. I reached out and grabbed Bendy's jacket with my right hand and began beating his shoulder with my left. Howard was up out of his chair and separated us.

'OK, lads, that's enough.'

The landlord appeared. 'Any problems, gentlemen?'

'No. Just a little disagreement. We're going. Get me the bill, will you? Gary, you take Bendy away now. I'll settle things here.'

'Right. Come on, Bendy lad.'

I heard them go, but I was looking down at the stain of red wine on the cloth, my mind racing but unable to think straight. It wasn't right, was it? Was it? But it could have been, for Christ's sakes. He was a man. She was a woman without a husband. He was alone with her every morning for forty years. Oh no. Oh no. Oh no. That's why she never came near our house. Nor Mam to hers. Oh Jesus. Jesus Christ. But what about Mam? She would guess, surely. And they never had any children after me. This was senseless. But they lived together. Slept in the same bed. And he was having sex with her, but not with Mam? And she knew. Oh no. No. No.

'Come on, Peter. I'll take you home.'

Home! Home! I couldn't go back. I couldn't face it. It wasn't my home anymore. It wasn't the one I knew.

In the event, I stayed at Howard's place. Clean linen, warm pyjamas. Howard phoned Mam to let her know I wouldn't be back until the morning. Before we went to bed, I asked Howard about Dad and Auntie Pauline.

I'd already begun to believe the rumour. Was it true? He didn't answer straight away, so the signs were not good.

'When you live in a small place like this, little incidents known to only a few people expand until it seems everybody knows them to be true or think they do. And once they're fixed in the folklore, they're difficult to shift, particularly if no one wants to disbelieve them. If you ask, *do I know this to be true?* then no, I don't. I've not seen anything to confirm it. However, you only have to sit in the bar at The Anchor or the stalls at the market to hear stories told by someone who was told something by someone else, and before you know it, a myth is created. Then, once most people believe it, it *has* to be true, doesn't it?'

'Do you believe it?' I wanted him to say it was untrue.

'What I know is that pretty well every Sunday for thirty years, your father went over to Mrs Dobson's and was there with her for a couple of hours. Was he being unfaithful to your mother? Was he a gardener or a lover? Like you, I know what I want to believe, but you can't stifle small-town gossip.'

I slept soundly that night, but it wasn't because of a mind at rest, but one dulled by too much alcohol. Morning would bring its revenge.

SUNDAY

Howard dropped me home, and I stood looking at the house before going in. It was only the day before I could have stood by that front gate and seen that house as mine. As home anyway. I knew its inhabitants. Mam and Dad. I knew its history, and I was a player. But now it had changed. I could no longer trust my version of what was inside. Once there was predictability, simplicity, love and faithfulness. Now I had to accept that these might have formed a veneer over quite a different life. I felt this house and those in it had betrayed me, and I was the victim of their deceit. I didn't want to go in there believing the worst that the previous night had revealed. But I had to go in. There was nowhere to run to. The people in there had not changed; it was only my view of their lives that had altered.

'Hello, Peter. How are you feeling?'

'So-so. A bit of a bad head.'

'Howard rang to say you were staying with him. Too much to drink. Rascals – the pair of you.'

'Did he say anything else?'

'No, it was a bit late.'

I looked at my mother. She had changed, hadn't she. People are not just what they are, but what they seem to others. Yet her hair hadn't changed; the slope of her shoulders was just the same. The quiet calmness of her gaze, that had not altered. And she still blinked plaintively behind her glasses. But did Mam know what I knew? What did I know? Had she assumed all along that I knew? Was I just stupid?

'How's Dad?' Dad. Who the hell was he now?

'Much the same.'

The same as what? I didn't know now.

'I'll just change and then pop in to see him.'

'Good lad.'

I had not been a good lad. Did she know about all that? The drinking? The women? I'd always felt it didn't matter what I did. My roots were sound. However I behaved, there would be a sanctuary in my early life. And that excuse, that support, had gone. Until this moment, family life had been a smooth ride. The three cogs that were me, Mam and Dad had moved in well-oiled togetherness. Now there was grit in there. Had Bendy fouled it up, or was he just the messenger? Who else believed this story? Was it a story – a product of Bendy's troubled mind – or could it be true? I couldn't ask Mam, and Dad was out of it. I wouldn't have asked them anyway. And sure as hell, I couldn't ask Auntie Pauline. Did she deserve to be called Auntie anymore?

★★★

When my mother had gone to church, I rang Maureen. It didn't take long. I always find it difficult to stretch out a conversation unless it's business. Maureen can, of course, and she did her best. She couldn't suspect anything about… could she?

Afterwards, I went to sit with Dad. I did not go into the bedroom then with the fear and sadness I had done earlier, but with an anger. I wanted to confront what I'd found out. I wanted to get Dad to confess. But he couldn't. He could only blow little bubbles from the side of his mouth and burp sweet sour breaths into my face. His eyes opened, and he saw me. He knew it was me; that's what I wanted to think. What was he thinking? Dad couldn't know I had changed, how let down I felt. I might hate him. But I didn't. Should I pity him, or should he pity me?

His eyes turned lethargically to one side.

'Do you want a drink?'

He wasn't going to reply. I had to get on with it. I put the plastic cup to his lips and reached my hand behind his head so that he could drink. I was frightened of breaking him. If it was hurting, I was sorry. I was hurting too, but he wasn't to know. It was too late to make any difference to him. But what about me?

He gave a grunt which I chose to believe was the sound of thanks. He lay back and closed his eyes. Another bubble came from his mouth, and I wiped it away with a tissue.

I needed to know if Dad fucked Auntie Pauline. Did he do it whilst I was out in the garden? Did he do it every Sunday morning while Mam was in church? That's what

I was thinking, and now I'd never know. Not from him. But I could go and see Auntie Pauline. Auntie fucking Pauline.

I left quite a bit of food on the plate. It was another of Mam's great Sunday roasts, but I couldn't eat it all.

'I'm sorry, Mam. I'm still a bit queasy from last night.'

'And you're going out again tonight. Can you cope?'

I'd forgotten that. A meal cooked by a good-looking lady, in her own house, with some hope of a leisurely lay afterwards. I'd usually kill for that. But what now? I might end up doing just what my dad did, betraying my wife to sleep with another woman. If I didn't go, I'd be stuck in with Mam. I would go; I was up for it.

When Mam had gone to Sunday school, I went up to sit with Dad. I had got used to his condition. It was Dad, not some croaking, farting living corpse. Then the fear came back. And of course, it was fear for me as well as fear for him.

I told him I was going out that night, a confession really. That in five or six hours I'd be cooped up in bed with a hot, healthy, throbbing body. Wouldn't he like to be there? Oh Christ, what a stupid thing to say.

Was this something I'd inherited from him? But if Dad was handing things down, he was handing me death too. And some day, I'd be a spluttering wreck like him. It's no wonder we do what we do.

★★★

Mam and I had afternoon tea in the back room with the telly and the lived-in chairs, not the front room where the doctor and Mr Baverstock were taken.

'You know, Mam, all those years Dad went to do Auntie Pauline's garden, you never came with us. How's that?'

'I went to church, and there was a lot to do in the house.'

But she didn't go out to work. She had all week to do the housework. She could have gone if she'd wanted.

'But she never came here either, did she?'

'No, she didn't.'

I knew Mam wouldn't lie – to anyone, not just me. Her being religious. I mean really Christian – kind, honest, truthful. She wouldn't lie to me, so all I had to do was ask whether my father, her husband, had been having a forty-year fling with a widow who had once been her best friend. Could I really ask that? I cleared my throat but still hadn't made up my mind to ask. She beat me too it.

'You see, a long time ago – you were about to go to secondary school – Pauline and me had a row – not a big row. Well, a disagreement anyway. Bitter, hurtful things were said. It doesn't matter what about. It's not very important now. We both said things we shouldn't. And the ill-feeling festered for quite a time. People are silly like that. All of us. We do the silliest things for the silliest reasons and then can't go back. Anyway, she stuck to her house, and I stuck to mine. Poor Pauline.

She did miss Harry so. She couldn't bring herself to leave the house very often. I often wondered then whether she didn't go out in case he came back and she wasn't there. It's a terrible thing to lose the one you love. Poor Pauline.'

Poor Pauline! Did Mam know what she was saying?

'But Dad still went to do her garden.'

'He'd promised Harry he'd look after her. I think your dad was there when Harry was injured. They took him off to the hospital, but he was dead before they picked him up. Your dad hasn't talked much about it, but over the years, bits of things have come out. So, I think he made a promise to see she was taken care of.'

I'll say!

'Does she know Dad's ill?'

'Oh yes. I've seen her a little more often once Dad stopped going up there. It seemed odd after all those years. It made me feel better. I felt I hadn't been very Christian. But I prayed for her, every week. All those years.'

She prayed for her husband's mistress!

'Did she ask to see him?'

'No. There was no need. Nothing to be said really.'

'She might have wanted to see him. To say goodbye.'

'She wouldn't have come here.'

And I still didn't know the truth. It could have been all innocent just as she said. Except she didn't say it was innocent. I wanted to believe it was. I couldn't believe Dad would behave like that. Yet I had.

★★★

My mouth was dry. I was nervous. I knocked on the door. What the hell was I doing here? I shouldn't be here. My head was spinning. I didn't want to be anywhere really. I couldn't make sense of it.

'Hi. I wasn't sure you'd come.'

Why did she say that? What did she know? Had Howard been gossiping?

'I wouldn't let a lady down.' My words seemed to struggle out, caught up in my throat.

'Come in.'

She had on a halter neck top and for some reason they turn me on. Not that I need a lot of turning. I've never understood it. They look great when they're on, but they're a bugger to get your hands into. No buttons, mind. Just over the head in one.

'Ta.'

'I was just making myself a gin and tonic. Can I get you something?'

I'd have preferred a beer.

'That'll do me.'

I'm not a great G and T man. The tonic really. Quinine, isn't it? Makes me wretch a bit. But I'd cope with one, if I sipped it. It's difficult to get used to sipping, not like beer where it goes down in gulps.

She went through to the back to get the drinks. I looked around a room that held no more interest than it did before.

'Nice place you've got.' Standard chat that.

'It's not my own. I rent. Don't know how long I'll be here.'

'Waiting to get back with your hubby then.'

There was a pause, and she came in with the glasses.

'I'll talk about my husband if you want to talk about your wife.'

She handed me a glass.

'Yeah. OK. You're right. Sorry.'

She was right. There are some things you don't talk about. Like politics with the customers. You'll usually get it wrong. Gave that bloke in Lincoln some real gung-ho stuff, only to find he'd got a CND sticker on his car. Don't think he ordered again. Bastard.

'It's difficult to get right, isn't it? Life I mean. You think you've got it sorted, then – bang – it all goes wrong,' said Sally.

She bloody knew, didn't she.

'I've always found it pretty straightforward. You work hard; you do well. You keep your nose clean; you don't get into trouble.'

'It's as easy as that, is it?'

'Well, perhaps not quite. But people bring it on themselves.'

'You're either very lucky or you're kidding yourself.'

'Maybe.'

'Let's eat. I've done a beef casserole. I could tell you're a beef man.'

Now that was a come-on if ever I heard one.

'Love it.'

'I got the wine from the hotel. Pour some out while I get the food.'

She was a good cook, no doubt about it. And a good talker too. Nothing personal but lots of stuff from the hotel and the neighbours. Whether it was the wine or her chat, I don't know, but I forgot about Dad. For afters, we had a little pudding she'd obviously bought somewhere, unless she'd pinched it from the hotel. I went to pour some more wine; the bottle was empty. I didn't notice her drink much. Bloody women. They sit there sipping away and they're on top of the world when you're beginning to slide off.

'You go and sit in the front while I just clear up here.'

I sat facing her front window. It was dark outside, but the sky was clear. I could see the reflection of her ceiling light in the glass, like it was in another room outside. And I could see my own reflection. Just my head, bobbing above the sill. I could see I was getting on a bit, with my short hair and fat face – no, not fat, plump. No, not plump either. Full. That's it. Full face. I wasn't the young lad who used to race around these streets on his bike. I'd come a long way since then. Made good. I wondered what happened to that bike. Was it in the shed? Dad's shed. Oh shit. I was brought back by the sound of clattering dishes from the back. She came through and drew the curtains over the window.

'Fancy a brandy?'

A short again! Why not?

'Just a little one.'

She gave me an old-fashioned look. As she sat next to me, she cradled her glass in her hand. I did the same. It felt comforting, the glass smooth and just occupying the ball of my hand. She took a sip, but I just looked into the oily brown liquid.

'What's the matter?' she asked.

'What do you mean?'

'I'd have thought by now your hands would have been all over me.'

And she was right. Normally I'd have tried it on by then. But I wasn't in the mood. I never thought I'd say that.

'Is that what you want?'

'It's not what *you* want?'

Women. Never answer a question.

'I've got things on my mind.'

'Can't you talk to someone about it?'

'Who?'

'Well, your mates. Howard. That's what I'd do.'

Yeah, well that's what women do. Bloody natter to each other about everything and everybody. Blokes don't do that.

'Do you ever see *your* parents now?'

I shouldn't have started. I knew I shouldn't. I should have kept my mouth shut. But once I had started, I knew it would all come out.

'No. They're still alive, but we don't get on.'

'Did you have a happy childhood?'

'No. Well, mixed. It's got to be, hasn't it? But there were some bad things.'

'Mine was great.'

I know there was Billy, but that didn't make my childhood bad, not the bits with Mam and Dad and the holidays and the shed and the bike. Dad's bike.

I don't believe this now, but I started to cry. It could have been the gin, the wine, the brandy, but it wasn't. I hadn't cried since I was very young, since my beach ball got blown out to sea at Southport. When the tide's out, the beach at Southport seems to go on forever. I watched as my ball sped away on the wind, growing smaller as it went, never to return. It seemed so cruel. Up to then, if anything went wrong in my life, Mam or Dad would put it right. But now something had happened that couldn't be put right. My precious ball had gone forever. Even when Billy died, I didn't cry, even though he'd gone forever. There were the nightmares, but I didn't cry. But I cried then. And she reached across, took my glass and snuggled my head against her shoulder. It probably wasn't very long, but I didn't seem to want to stop. Great heaving sobs and my nose running. I leant away from her and struggled to get my hanky.

I looked at her top, her halter top. It had my snot all over it; a damp patch nearly reached her breast. I looked at it with none of the feelings I had grown used to.

'I'm sorry.' I had to clear my throat.

'That's OK.' Her voice was soft, not like the voice I had expected when I walked into The Anchor the other night. 'Come upstairs and get cleaned up.'

I followed her up the stairs. And yes, I looked at her legs and how they disappeared beneath her skirt, at the creases at the back of her knees. And yes, I saw her hips move from side to side as she took the steps. And yes, I thought she was a very attractive woman.

She ran some water in the washbasin and washed my face for me. Just like Mam used to do. And she dried it, dabbing the soft towel, warm where it had been on the radiator. Not like Mam used to do it.

'Better now?' I nodded and went onto the landing. The door to her room was open, not the mean back room she'd taken me to before, but her own bedroom. The duvet on the bed was turned back; the table lamp gave the room soft light and warm shadows. She pushed me gently in the back.

'Go on down. This isn't the time.'

And she was right. They always know, women. We went down to her front room, and I saw the time on her clock.

'Christ I must be going. I promised my mam I wouldn't be late.'

Then I realised what I'd said and looked at her. She laughed back. Not a mocking laugh but a friendly, gentle, comforting noise which made me smile at my own condition.

We stood by the closed front door for a moment. She pulled me to her, and I felt her body warm and full against mine. It was a woman's body, but she was not offering it to me, and I did not want it.

'You'll sort it out. Don't worry. It'll all be better in the morning.'

That's what Mam always said when I was poorly. But this time it wasn't. It was worse.

★★★

When I got in, Mam was in the back room. She seemed different.

'Hello, Mam. Are you OK? How's Dad?'

'He's gone. He died about seven-fifteen. The doctor's been.'

I hadn't expected it like that. I'd expected to be there. I'd built up to it. To be there when he breathed his last breath. To have said goodbye before he went. To tell him how much I loved and respected him. To hold Mam and comfort her. This was the picture I had created even before I came to stay. But now he had gone without me, when I was with Sally. I had gone out before seven and he was alive; now I'd come back, and he was dead.

'Is he still upstairs?' His body I meant, of course.

'Yes. Dr Jamieson will arrange for the undertakers to come first thing in the morning.'

'Did he say anything?' Dad, not Dr Jamieson.

'He asked for you. I didn't know where you were. I rang Mrs Watson to see if she knew where you were. Howard answered, but he didn't know.'

I looked at Mam. She was looking straight at me. She knew I had lied. And I knew that whatever I said next she would think was a lie.

'I'm sorry, Mam.' But it wasn't a lie.

I didn't want her to look at me, not eye contact. She'd know I was lying. I was her son. And I was Dad's son too.

'Should I go and see him?' Of course I should.

'I'll come with you.'

She held out her hand and put it around mine like she did on that first day at school, that first ride at on the merry-go-round at New Brighton, that first visit to the dentist. She had to let go as we climbed the stairs, they were too narrow for two people abreast, but she took hold of my hand again when we got to the bedroom door and eased me through. I didn't know what to expect; I'd never seen a dead body before. I could see he had changed. His face was no longer his; there was less tension in his muscles. I could believe he was at peace. His hands were under the bedsheets. He was no longer on his half of the bed but lying centrally as if in a cotton coffin. Surely Mam would not sleep with him tonight.

'Where will you sleep, Mam?'

'I've made up a camp bed in the back bedroom. I'll be fine. I've put a hot water bottle in it. To air it, you know.'

How she could be so calm, so practical, I couldn't understand. I had expected her to grieve, even for me to be embarrassed by it. But she had seen him like this for months. Had all the grief drained out of her? I had to admit I was relieved it was all so unemotional; I would not have wanted to witness her distress and not give her comfort. Had something been drained out of me too? Did I not have the ability to be emotional? Where had that gone? Did I ever have it?

'Would you like a few moments with him alone? I know you were close.'

Was I close to Mam?

'Yes. That would be…'

Nice, good, right. I'd lost the right word.

'I'll go down and put the kettle on. Don't stay too long. It's gone a little cold in here. I turned the radiator off. There's no point in keeping the room warm.'

I nearly said: *No leave it on, he'll get cold*. How stupid was that?

'I won't be long.'

I pulled up a chair alongside his bed just level with his head. Those ears can't hear. But it's what I would have done if he was still alive. Sentences began to form, then fell apart. If I said all the things I wanted to say; all the things I'd been saving up to say, I would have been a long time. But I knew my thoughts, my emotions, my speech would have given up on me. No matter how much I had intended to reminisce about the times we spent together – making things in the garage, trying to catch fish with just a line and a hook, climbing up to the top of Leaden Hill – these things would stay locked up inside me. There was no one there to share them with. He'd gone.

I should have said things to him before this. I had intended to, but I kept putting it off until it was too late. I thought he was wonderful; he'd given me every encouragement, every chance in life. True, he hadn't paid for me to go to a good school, but he'd saved for us to have annual family holidays, a fine spread for Christmas dinner, nice presents at birthdays, decent clothes when some of my mates had hand-me-downs. And I had taken it for granted. I didn't think it was the time to confront him over Auntie Pauline.

It wasn't true, was it? Was it?

MONDAY

I awoke to the realisation that what I had anticipated had happened and couldn't be undone. The landscape had changed. I could no longer say things to my father that I had stored up over weeks. I assumed that, in time, the gap in my life would fill, and things would gradually return to normal. But not this morning. It was too raw. Dad – his body – was in the next room. Deaf to me. His past – or his version of it – was dead to me.

Breakfast was a subdued affair; there was tension, but was it between Mam and me, or just within me? Plates were placed on the table rather more carelessly than usual; tea was poured from a greater height. Crockery was cleared to the kitchen, and the sound of plates knocking against each other in the sink seemed amplified. But these were the sounds that dominated; between Mam and me, there was little conversation beyond the practical. What could I say? I had lied to my mother, and she knew it. It had meant a troubled night in bed.

I should have offered comfort, but I couldn't bring

myself to embrace her. She had never been a huggy person – ever. True, she held my hand, mopped my brow, stroked my back, but I don't recall a close hug. Had that absence of physical contact affected me? It was a bit too late to think of that now. I asked what she wanted to do that day. The usual routines were gone. Dad did not need feeding. Clothes were already on the washing line. What time did Mam get up?

'What's happening today, Mam?' I didn't suppose there would be a diary entry.

'The undertakers are coming at ten o'clock. To collect the body.'

To collect Dad! As though they were coming for any other reason. Then came a plan I wasn't expecting.

'When they've gone, I'm going to sort out all Dad's clothes and send them to the church to go to Africa.'

'But he's only just… gone.'

'If I don't do it now, while you're here, I'll let it drag out.'

There was something in her manner that had changed. It seemed that now that Dad had gone, she had finally come out into the open, stronger, more determined, more independent. Had all this been building up inside her, and now that he had gone, it burst out?

'If you come across anything I might like, put it to one side.'

'Yes. I understand. I'll just send his clothes; you won't want those. I'll check the pockets. I'll leave the clothes on the bed; you can bag them up for me. You can go through the drawers later. For now, you can go to the garage and see what can go from there.'

'From the garage! You can't empty that.'

'It's got to be done, Peter. There's nothing in there we can use.'

I unlocked the double doors with the key that hung on a hook on the edge of the crockery cabinet in the kitchen. I noted how smoothly the lock responded to the key. Pulling the doors open revealed the ordered world that was Dad's – and mine for a time. Working surfaces along two sides – on one a vice, a circular saw, a chisel sharpener. Above them were several racks holding screwdrivers, chisels and other tools whose names I could not remember. The chisel blades were covered by paper coverings of various origins – wrappers from chocolate bars and biscuits, pieces of waxed bags that had held bread – all designed to keep the metal free of damp. One of the sleeves had dropped onto the bench below, revealing a blade that had already begun to rust. On the face of the wooden rack above each was written the size of the blade. At the far end was another bench under which was a pile of plastic bags which had once held compost and groceries. Above it and attached to the wall were racks of small plastic drawers for holding nails, screws, bolts, washers and wall plugs, each labelled methodically by size and gauge, head type and type of metal. A pile of old tobacco tins – Golden Virginia, Three Nuns, Players – were stacked on top of them, holding the items that didn't fit into this template – fuses, cup hooks, drawing pins and cable clips. Around pairs of hooks were coiled miscellaneous lengths of power cable. Above all this was a wooden shelf supported by four brackets. On it was a motley collection of biscuit and chocolate tins, containing what, I couldn't remember, although I had a feeling the coronation one held pieces of sandpaper and suspected that two others contained wall plaster and paintbrushes. I knew the biggest contained all those items that were left over from jobs or found on the floor – odd drawing pins, single brackets, pieces of plastic with no discernible use.

While I was in there, the undertakers came. I could see their vehicle pull up at the roadside. There was nothing on its sides to indicate what it was. It's not the thing you advertise. I didn't want to get involved, though I felt I should. I went back into the kitchen as Mam let them in. She showed them up the stairs, and after some muffled sounds, they came down with a stretcher with belts holding Dad's body in place. They struggled to maintain dignity and balance on the narrow stairway. I could see all this from the kitchen where I was hiding – yes, I was hiding.

Mam stood on the doorstep as they put the stretcher in their vehicle – it was hardly a hearse. She waited until it drove away and a little longer as it went to the bottom of Wellworth Road to turn round to go back up to the chapel of rest at the other end of the village. I had no idea what she was thinking as she held this vigil. As the van turned off the road out of sight, she glanced in the opposite direction. It was the route Dad would have taken each Sunday morning as he cycled up to Auntie Pauline's to do her garden. What the hell was she thinking?

'There's work to be done, Peter. Let's have a cup of tea first, eh?'

After she'd taken her first sip, she said, 'When you've

got a moment, could you pop over to Auntie Pauline's and ask her to come to the funeral? Tell her I would be glad if she could come.'

I held my cup with both hands so that she couldn't see me shaking.

'Yes. Of course. But why?'

'She and your dad were very close for many years. I'm sure she'd like to pay her respects. And Harry would have liked that as well.'

Very close!

'But you and her weren't that close, were you?'

'Not for a while. That row was silly really. I regret it now. It was not necessary, but we made it up and we're closer now.'

I took another sip, wondering if there was more to come. If there was, I wasn't going to hear it now.

'I'll go tomorrow. We may have more details then.'

'You go back to the shed while I go upstairs and make a start on the clothes.'

Back in the garage, I stood for a while thinking, but nothing coherent. The contents came to my rescue. Across the roof spars above were pieces of timber of varying cross sections and lengths. Alongside them, odd lengths of copper pipe. And in this Aladdin's cave, miracles of construction and maintenance had been performed. Once I had been part of it, but now I could barely assemble a flatpack bookcase.

Along the third wall was the gardening equipment. A mower (manual of course) and a small roller. Forks and spades, rakes and hoes, all free of soil, were raised above the floor, held in place by metal clips.

Lying against the garden tools was his bike, black and sturdy, front and back lamps driven by a dynamo on the back wheel. I raised the bike up by its seat and turned the back wheel using a pedal. The dynamo whirred and the lamps lit up, illuminating the far wall of the garage. When I stopped pedalling, the lights dimmed and eventually went out. It was like Dad's final days. Dead!

Above the wheel was a platform on which I had travelled, clinging onto Dad's rough tweed jacket. To Auntie Pauline's!

I thought I had managed to put her out of my mind, but there she was again. But she hadn't been in *here*, not this private den of reliability and dependability, untainted by lust and betrayal. Dad. Surely not Auntie Pauline! Surely!

Was there something I could take away as a souvenir? There was a tool tray with side compartments and a central handle which he used to carry tools to do jobs in the house. Inside each compartment was a mixture of small tools that seemed outsiders in this well-organised place. I picked out a screwdriver with a bulbous wooden head designed to make handling easier. The wood was comfortably worn, smooth to the touch, and the handle nestled comfortably into my palm. Dad's hands would have worn this smooth. Someone had scored two initials in the handle. EC. That's Dad OK. On half a turn of the handle were two more initials, PD. Not Pauline Dobson! Dad wouldn't have done that. His initials and Auntie Pauline's, together. It was too sentimental for him. Mam mustn't see this. I'd take it with me when I went home.

Taking great care to lock the garage securely, I returned

to Mam in the house. I'd brought the screwdriver out with me. I put the tool in my jacket pocket; I could put it in my case later. At the bottom of the stairs was one black bin bag.

'That doesn't seem much, Mam.'

'I've bagged it all to save you. It was easier to put them straight in the bags, and you might not have wanted to touch Dad's clothes. I brought that one down. There are four more upstairs. Will you bring them down later, after we've had a cup of tea?'

While we were drinking our tea in the back room, I tried to find out more about what she was thinking.

'Did you find it difficult to do the clear-out?'

She looked out of the window at the back garden before replying. 'Lots of things in life are difficult. But some must be done. I think Dad would have understood. He liked things orderly, didn't he?'

'What will you do with all the things in the garage? You can't dump *them*, surely.'

'I had the idea of putting a notice up in the church saying I was having a sale of garage items one Saturday morning. Anyone could come and have what they wanted with donations going to the church. I'm sure Tommy Johnson would come and help and make sure people paid a fair price. He worked with Dad for years, so I can rely on him.'

'Johnson. Was that Isabel Johnson's dad? Don't do it while I'm here. I think I would find it hard to take.'

'I won't. It's not urgent.'

'You could put a notice in the community hall and the Legion and the local pubs.'

'You know I don't like going into the pubs.'

Not like me, eh.

'Perhaps Mr Johnson would do it for you. Did you find anything I might want upstairs?'

'There's a cardboard box on the bed. Take what you want.'

There weren't many items in the box. There were several ties, two of which seemed military, so I took those. I also took a cap badge, a medal ribbon and, most important of all, his War Medal, not a special medal, but special to me nevertheless. The metal finish was a bit tarnished, but I would clean it up when I got home. I didn't suppose William would be interested in this.

I put them all, along with the initialled screwdriver, in my travelling case. I decided to send the whole box home with Maureen. I took the bin bags downstairs, but it took me two trips.

Mam and I decided that, after lunch, I could take them to the community hall where the Salvation Army would pick them up. Africa might have to wait.

Five bags were too cumbersome to take in one go, so I took three first. On the way back, I decided to walk back through the playing fields, although that wasn't the direct route. It was here we used to play when young before venturing further afield as we became more courageous – and reckless.

When I reached the far end, I sat on a low wall looking across the road. When I was very young – a toddler I suppose – we used to live in one of a row of small two-up two-down cottages facing the fields. They had been demolished years ago. The front doors led straight onto the street, and I don't remember much of a garden at the back. The walls must have been thin as I'm sure I heard the woman next door shouting at her kids. What was her name now – Wilkinson? Parkinson? Wilson? None of these, but lost now. For little children, grown-ups don't often have names, only a presence. There didn't seem to be a husband. Did the war claim another casualty? It could have been our family. Or was she abandoned?

I had very few memories of living there since we soon moved to one of the council houses where Mam and Dad lived the rest of their lives. That new house, our family home, overwhelmed all earlier memories.

The cottages had been knocked down soon after we left. In their place came a filling station of a brand long since taken over and now abandoned to weeds and dust. Why do disused filling stations have such a disturbing effect? Is it that they declare loss in such a stark way? Disused petrol pumps like statues, symbols of another life. This short-lived newcomer left its mark on the village, mainly with the abandoned polystyrene trays and plastic bags now skating around the forecourt at the bidding of every breeze.

Up the Wellworth Road, just beyond the redundant pumps, was a chip shop. It was from here that most of the litter came. The shop used to be Horrocks, the newsagent. Gordon used to deliver his papers for a while, but he didn't like the cold mornings. Mrs Horrocks caught us shoplifting once and chased us off. She knew who we were but didn't tell our parents. Did she? It was only liquorice sticks for God's sake.

The chip shop survived by serving the new houses

on Cooksley Road and the late-night returnees from The Anchor. The out-of-town retail parks were drawing the residual trade away – cheaper petrol and more shops. It had seen off Mr and Mrs Horrocks, who couldn't compete any more than the petrol station could. I traipsed back to Mam's.

After a rest and another cup of Mam's tea, I retraced my steps to the community hall with the last two bags of clothes and a shopping list from Mam. While in the supermarket, I bought a paper – sorry, Mr Horrocks – and several packets of fags – sorry, Mrs Horrocks.

When I got back, Mrs Riley – Freda – from next door, was with Mam. There was a pronounced silence when I came in, and the neighbour soon left. She had moved in when the Smiths left, and I had always seen her as a stranger, an intruder even.

The rest of the day was spent uneasily. Perhaps we should have reminisced, but how could I do that without Auntie Pauline intruding? Mam was subdued – which I expected – and calm. She'd just lost her husband of fifty years, so I anticipated a tearful revisiting of their past lives. But there was none of that. I suppose Mam had been expecting this for many months, had spent hours feeding and washing Dad; so much must have been said between them. Did she ever say goodbye? Surely, we all put that off, hoping it will go away, until it's too late and the moment is gone. Did she ever talk about love? Lots of people do so without knowing what it means. Did they ever talk about Auntie Pauline?

During the evening, we sat uncomfortably quiet and talking awkwardly in turn. I wanted to sleep, to lose myself in unconsciousness, but didn't want to make the first move for bed in case I reinforced my position as a bad son.

TUESDAY

I'd slept of course but could convince myself I'd lain awake all night, tossing from one uncomfortable position to another, from one uncomfortable thought to another. I'd got up twice: once for a drink when my mouth and throat were dry from alcohol and once for a pee to shed the tea that Mam had made before we went to bed.

At breakfast that morning, the talking was functional. Later, we went to see Dad in the chapel of rest and discuss the funeral arrangements with the undertaker and Mr Baverstock. Dad was to be buried. We'd have to choose a coffin. Mam had kept back some of his clothes from the cull the day before. He was to be buried in his wedding suit. Most people would have outgrown theirs, but the disease that killed him reunited him with his past. Mam had ironed one of his white shirts and a regimental tie. Would he wear shoes and socks?

The short walk to the chapel of rest took us down the road at the side of the precinct that led to the council estate at the back of our house. On a corner of a side road was the joinery shop where Dad had spent his working life. The gates to it were open, and someone was talking to the driver of a large waggon which was delivering planks of wood. I stopped to look inside, paying some respect, I thought, honouring a life of honest toil. They'd had their money's worth out of Dad.

Further down the side road was the undertaker's office and, next to it, the chapel of rest, discreetly out of sight of the shoppers in the precinct going about their lives, not wanting to think about death. We went into the office to be greeted (greeted!) by Mr Stevens, the son of Stevens & Son. He wore his dark suit and tie like a uniform.

How did he do that job? Death and grief every day! Didn't he ever want to get away?

His father had been a drinking pal of Dad's at the Legion, one of the many who had found in the club a community devoid of politics and religion, class even, their only link, survival when their friends did not. But Mr Stevens senior had died last year; no one, it seemed, however well connected, was immune from death. He had been supervising at Billy's funeral, and I thought he had looked at me accusingly, but then for weeks, every time I walked through the village, I thought every glance was a spotlight of blame.

Mr Stevens took us through a side door from his office into the chapel. Mam handed over Dad's funeral clothes. Dad – it had to be Dad – lay straight and flat, so obviously dead, so obviously not him, and yet it was his body. I didn't cry; I thought I should have. Mam didn't cry; I thought she would have.

It had come, the moment I knew would come for

the last forty years. It would only come once, and now it had gone. Another marker on my own road. I knew I should be deeply upset, but my strongest feeling was that I should feel worse. Mam stood at the foot of the bed and prayed. She put her hands together, closed her eyes and spoke silently. I looked at her for a moment, unable to judge what she was feeling, and for an instant, hoped she was praying for me too. I turned my eyes to the bed and saw only one thing.

Goodbye, Dad.

I knew they were inadequate words, but I needed to say something, and my ability to create anything more profound had deserted me. I had said them silently; only I could hear. No one else. Not even Dad.

Mr Stevens declared, 'I've spoken to Mr Baverstock, and we think two-thirty on Friday would be the best if that's all right with you.'

He was making the running as though he was tired of listening to relatives whose capacity for decision-making had been blunted by grief. I wondered whether he had any feeling or whether he was just selling too, like me on the road.

'We'd like to choose a coffin.'

Mr Stevens smiled. 'Come through here. I've got just the thing.'

He pointed to a coffin laid out on two trestles. It was beautifully made. A good wood. The handles were in solid brass and a name plate was fixed to the top which was propped up against one side. The inside was lined with a soft white cloth awaiting a body.

'What do you think?' asked Mr Stevens.

'It's beautiful.' Mam stroked the brass plate.

'I can get that inscribed before Friday, if you tell me what you want it to say.'

I could see the quality of the workmanship. It was difficult to see the joints so finely had they been cut. I ran my fingers over where the side pieces butted against the ends. There was no feeling of a join.

'It's best oak,' boasted Mr Stevens.

'I'm not sure we could afford this. We've…' Mam paused. 'I've got some savings in a special account at the Post Office but…'

I was just about to tell Mam not to worry about the cost, not knowing what it was. I would have paid anything for that coffin.

'It won't cost anything, Mrs Carter. Eric saw to it all.'

'You mean Dad paid for it.'

'No, Peter. Not just that. He made it himself.'

My eyes filled, but I held back the tears. The old bugger. The clever old bugger.

'It took him a long time, but it's a wonderful job. Over the years he came down here for the odd hour or two, and he and my father talked away while he did this. The wood came from Bennetts; the fittings came through us; and Eric paid for them. Trade prices of course.'

I thought he was selling. But he wasn't.

'My father used to tell him: "It's too good to go in the ground. I ought to put it in my window, Eric." And Eric said: "Only if you'll have me inside it.".'

'When did he start doing it?' Mam asked.

'About two years ago.'

Mam said no more, but she must have worked out he would have known he'd got cancer then. He'd been going to the hospital behind her back. And going to the undertakers too. I imagined Dad could hear this tribute to his skills as he lay in the next room and wondered what else he was thinking.

As we retraced our steps, I noted the two buildings that had marked Dad's later life: the undertaker's which confirmed his death and, across the road, the wood shop which defined his working life. How close they were, like life and death, so close.

Over at the church, Mam and Mr Baverstock chose the hymns and the prayers. She'd had suggestions written down, and the two of them talked about things with a familiarity which eluded me. Periodically, Mr Baverstock brought me into the conversation.

Again, I thought he was selling. But he wasn't.

Over a lunch of fish fingers, Mam and I were subdued. Since then, I have invented all the things I should have said, wanted to say, but didn't. Then, they would not come. And she found no eloquent words to say either. Like most people, we took refuge in the ordinariness of life. She said one thing which was memorable, although it, too, sprang from the mechanics of death.

'Peter, love,' I was encouraged by that opening as it seemed to forgive my sins of Sunday, 'remember I asked you to ask Auntie Pauline to the funeral. Well, would you go up this afternoon and invite her?'

I agreed, too shocked to ask why she couldn't do it herself, still less why she wanted to do it at all.

'And, Peter, ask if she'd like to go to the chapel of rest, to see Dad.'

★★★

I stood at the corner of the lane to Sally's house and the road to Auntie Pauline's in no doubt as to which one I preferred to take, but there was no real choice. I had a duty to my mother, and I was drawn to this woman who might have been my father's lover. It was inescapable that we should meet.

The small front garden was well kept, tidy and ready for winter.

I'd never called her by her Christian name alone. Always Auntie. Auntie Pauline. Two words, one person, but she'd changed now inside my head. She'd become a different person. I needed to meet her. I needed to confront her. To confront *it*. I took a deep breath, like when you jump into a pool or walk into a client's shop. I rang the bell, and though the man in me made me wait, the boy in me wanted to run away. I heard faint noises behind the door and then the handle turning. And there she was. She was smaller than I had expected, taller than Mam, but then, who isn't? Her hair was grey and her skin lined. Nothing to suggest she had been an attractive woman. She looked at me but said nothing. Her face changed as I looked at it, but I wasn't sure what it was revealing.

'Hello, Auntie Pauline. It's Peter. Peter Carter.'

Auntie! I wasn't going to use it. But I'd lost it, hadn't I. It was going to be Auntie Pauline forever. She looked at me, seeming to gather her thoughts.

'Oh. Yes. Of course. You've grown.'

What a daft remark. I was thirty years older.

'Well, it's been a long time.'

'Yes. Come in. Come in. I'm sorry I couldn't see you against the sunlight.'

I passed very close to her in the hallway and felt myself hating her, an unreasoned but noticeable hate. I thought she went to hug me, but I could have been mistaken.

'Go through to the parlour.'

I hadn't heard that word for a while.

'Sit down, won't you. Would you like a cup of tea? Haven't got anything stronger, I'm afraid.' She smiled bleakly.

'No thanks. I've got some bad news.'

'About Eric?'

'Yes. He passed away on Sunday night.'

And I was in that house you can see next door. Eating and drinking with… my lover?

'I do know. Your mum sent a note yesterday. It was pushed through the door. It might have been Freda who brought it.'

She said nothing immediately but turned to stand in front of the French window overlooking the garden. I could see the garden beyond her. It was fuller now, the bushes more developed and overhanging the lawn in places. The grass was losing its summer greenness, but it was well looked after. The circular flower bed in the middle was still there with a weeping willow occupying its centre. I remembered us digging that out.

She lowered herself into the armchair beside the

window, and I could see the tears in her eyes. She took a handkerchief from her pinafore and blew her nose. My hand wanted to reach out and hold hers in a spasm of consolation, but my mind wouldn't let it.

'He was so good to me. For all those years.'

What was I to make of that?

'He said he'd promised Harry he'd look after you.'

And how!

'And he did. Harry would have been so proud of him.'

She looked beyond me, and I had to turn. There was a photograph of two young soldiers. Dad and Harry. I barely knew which was which, so young were they and so fuzzy the picture. And there was a picture of me about ten, with a woman – it had to be Auntie Pauline.

'I'm going to put the kettle on. Are you sure you won't have a cup?'

There was nothing to hate in this little old woman. Every emotion had seemed genuine. There was no hint of anything other than the simplest, purest feelings.

'Yes. OK. Milk. One sugar. Ta.'

She came back into the room while the tea brewed. 'Your family must be quite grown up now. William, isn't it? And Claire. Eric used to show me their photographs. Lovely children they seemed. Harry and I said we'd have two children, a boy and a girl. No more. Not that you can choose these things. And it wasn't to be.'

She reached for her hankie and went to get the cups. They came on a tray with a plate of chocolate digestives. The surface of the tea shuddered as she handed me the cup.

I cleared my throat. 'Mam hopes you'll be able to come to the funeral. It's on Friday at half-past two. At the churchyard.'

Auntie Pauline looked a little surprised. 'Yes. I'd like that. I'll send some flowers.'

'No. No flowers. Donations to the Legion. That's what he wanted.'

'Yes. That's nice.' She looked out of the window. 'There may be a few blooms left out there. I'll put a few on the grave afterwards.'

I didn't want anything from this garden on Dad's grave. Not after...

Not after what? I tried to imagine her lying in bed enjoying the things I had enjoyed. And then I had to think of Dad enjoying them too. It didn't make sense. It didn't ring true. But why should it? I had constructed a picture of Dad to meet my own needs. I'd robbed him of some of his own personality. It didn't ring true because I didn't want it to be true. Did he really have a life, separate from me, separate from Mam? The bastard. How could he do that?

'He's in the chapel of rest. Would you like to see him?'

After a long pause, she said, 'No. No. I don't think I could.'

She said it as though she had made up her mind before this moment.

I said, 'I understand,' but I didn't.

'Will Maureen be there? And the children.'

'At the chapel of rest? No. No.'

'I meant the funeral.'

'Oh. Yes. Of course. They're coming over on Thursday. Staying a couple of days.'

'Good. I'd like to meet them.'

I couldn't really see myself introducing her to Maureen: I'd like you to meet Auntie Pauline; she used to shag Dad every Sunday morning. Christ this was too complicated. I wanted it all to go away.

'I must go. I don't want to leave Mam on her own.'

'Remember me to her. Give her my love.'

'I will. See you Friday.' Not Sunday.

In the small hallway she reached out to touch me, her hand on mine. I felt a faint squeeze. Was she touching Dad for the last time?

★★★

I didn't want to go home. Even the word home had been undermined. I struck off along Leaden Hill Road. I knew where it would take me, but I couldn't turn myself back. My mind was confused, what with Auntie Pauline and Mam and Sally. I just wanted to race ahead to be clear of them.

I strode briskly past Burton's Farm, except it wasn't a farm anymore. No abandoned machinery with odd spikes sticking out, no heaps of manure, no barking dogs, no chickens strutting about. It was all manicured, farm buildings once weathered, now repointed and clean, a cobbled forecourt on which were parked a car and a jeep. The road frontage, which was once an irregular hedge, was now a neat stone wall curving inwards to a wrought-iron gate at the entrance. On one of the gate's pillars was a signboard announcing: *Burton's Rest*.

I carried on at pace, around the bend with the electricity pylon in its elbow. We'd tried to climb it once, but a farmhand chased us off. Billy must have been with us, because after he died, we weren't so adventurous. Eventually, I came to the slight incline as the road rose over the bridge across the railway line. The railway tracks were separated from the surrounding farmland by a thick hawthorn hedge. Through a break in it and over the bridge ran the road to Leaden Hill. I can recollect being taken there by Dad; he on his bike, me on the pillion behind, hanging onto his jacket. Dad used to sit me on the parapet of this bridge to watch the train approaching and lift me off at the last minute before the bridge was enveloped in steam.

We came there when we were young, when there were six of us. And I was there again, like so many times before, leaning over the coping stones of the bridge, looking at the railway line below. Sometimes we'd wait for a train to come and thrill to its sheer power as it made the ground shake, ducking down below the parapet as the steam came rushing up. They were still steam then, when we played there. We used to lean out to see how far we could see into the tunnel beneath the bridge before scrambling down the earth bank at the end of the brickwork. We were told not to go there, but we took no notice; it was exciting. There we put copper coins on the track to have them hammered flat by the heavy wheels. What would they buy then? There we treated the rails like a tight rope, holding our arms out at right angles to our bodies like the acrobats we'd seen when the circus came to Cooksley. And we would use the sleepers as springboards as we hopped from one to the other; it soon became a competition, with Bendy being the champion with eight leaps all on his right leg. I think I managed five. As soon as we could feel an oncoming train, we would rush to the safety of the bushes alongside the track. To be safe of course, but to be hidden too; we didn't want the local bobby to know we were there and be denied our secret pleasures.

I looked into the distance, the track now devoid of rails and converted into a trail for ramblers, undisturbed now by trains. But it was still possible to imagine the rails tapering to a point. I knew where those tracks went; they went away. Away from Eldon to somewhere else, somewhere better; it didn't matter where. Just not here, where Dad worked for a pittance; not here, where a night out was pictures and chips in wherever; not here, where Billy died.

Billy was younger than us and one of his legs was rendered useless by a bout of polio. There were lots of childhood illnesses then – chickenpox, measles, scarlet fever, TB, mumps – and any one of us could have caught them. Most of us had had bouts of some of them; I had chickenpox. With polio, Billy had drawn the short straw. He couldn't run, and when we played football, he had to go in goal. He never complained, never asked for favours even when he struggled. We admired him for that. It was why he was one of us.

When we went on the railway line it took some time for Billy to get down, the steep muddy slope an obstacle.

But he always made it. And we always waited until he could join us. The journey up the slope was more difficult, and we had to be patient while he struggled his way up to join us, pulling on the small shrubs that populated the embankment.

We used to go inside the dark tunnel, shouting, so that our echoes came back from the brick ceiling, daring each other to go right through to the other side where a bright semicircle beckoned. On one occasion it was different, and I had to confront it in the hope it could be laid to rest; so I could forget it and get on with my life, just as I'd confronted Auntie Pauline, but I'd bottled that. I looked down and relived the whole episode. We had all gone inside, shouting, and whistling but, on hearing an oncoming train, rushed to the safety of the daylight. We all did, except Billy, at first. Finally, he did come out, but on the opposite side of the tracks to us. We called him over.

Come on, Billy. Over here.

We could hear the train coming, sense the vibration in the track.

Come on, Billy. There's plenty of time.

Who was it that shouted? We all did. Some more than others. I shouted. But Gordon shouted most.

Come on, Billy.

And Billy came. He tripped over a rail, his gammy leg making him lose his balance. The train hit him. There was a squealing of brakes, a rattling of wheels, hissing, creaking, banging. I can hear them now. And I can still hear another sound; it came from Billy just before he was hit. I don't remember words, just cries. But nothing from us; language had deserted us under the horror of what had just happened.

Come on.

It was Gordon again, but not to Billy now. To us. We knew, didn't we, that we couldn't help Billy. Something awful had happened that couldn't be undone, like my beach ball blowing along the sands at Southport. And we ran, each making his own noise inside, scrambling up the earth banks, grabbing the hawthorn bushes and scratching our hands. Onto the road and away, leaving the shouting, adult voices now, echoing in the tunnel below. We ran to the security of the oak tree in Burton's field, hidden and safe in its branches, pulling back into the foliage as the ambulance and police car raced by. We must have stayed away for ages, until it got dark at least. We didn't say much to each other, only to ourselves, inside, lying along thick branches, wrapping our arms around and pressing our bodies to the bark, seeking something solid for support. And then we went home, Gordon and me together. Where else to go? Sergeant Pinnock was there, looking huge. Mam and Dad looked awful. I did not need them to tell me some terrible thing had happened. I knew, but I didn't know what next. Prison perhaps. If they had told me to jump in the river, I think I'd have done it. I said Gordon had shouted. Next door, he said we'd all shouted, and he was right, but I couldn't take the blame. It was too big.

Later, in the bath, I washed a piece of soft debris from my hair. Billy's flesh, I thought. What else? I scooped it out of the bath water with a tooth mug and flushed it down the toilet.

Goodbye, Billy.

Down the drain. You'd had ten years of life. What would you have done with more? What had I done?

So, if Billy was one of the reasons I wanted to get away, it was not because I couldn't face living near the scene of his death, seeing his parents, his sister, although they left the village soon after. It was that I didn't want to die here, like him. There had to be more. Is that why Gordon went away? Why hasn't Howard gone? Or Bendy, or Gary? Can they be happy here where I could not?

I looked up the road towards Leaden Hill. Dad had ridden up there on his bike with me on the back many times. Just round the bend the road began to climb, and sometimes he had to get off and push. On the left-hand side of the slope were the ruins of an old cottage. Even then it was a wreck. No roof or window frames, thick spiky brambles preventing entry through the door.

Further on, just before the road opened onto the moorland, the banks on either side of the road, formed when the road was pushed up through the hillside, were covered with primroses. Not the whole year round, of course, but long enough for us to see them as a permanent feature. We called it Primrose Hill. Just me and Dad, our private name.

The primroses wouldn't be out yet. Too early.

At the top of the slope, the road left the wooded green of the valley and crossed some moorland. On the right-hand side, beyond a five-barred gate, ran a rough path. It led up to the top of Leaden Hill, zigzagging as it went to ease the severity of the slope. Dad left his bike chained to the gate, and we climbed up to the top, sometimes struggling for breath. From the top you could see for miles around – five counties on a clear day, so the legend went, but not many people could name them. There was no sign of human habitation at the top, only a few rocks, most being handy to sit on and a few large enough to shelter behind if the wind was brisk. If humans had ever built there, their descendants had cleared all the evidence over generations, to build their own houses, I supposed. Perhaps the cottage on the road below.

Dad usually brought a pack of home-made sandwiches, a piece of fruit, a pop bottle full of tap water and, just for me, a bar of chocolate. While we sat up there on the rocks eating our picnic, he used to tell me tales of the war, but I suspect now they were made up or at least exaggerated; they wouldn't be tales otherwise.

One visit stands out more than the others and not just because it was the last one we took together. Dad had finished his sandwiches and reached for his cigarettes. He always kept them in an old tobacco tin which snapped shut and kept them dry. He had a lighter made from an old bullet casing from the look of it. Whenever he bought a new packet of fags, he emptied them into this tin and made sure his lighter had fuel in it. With his usual ritual, he took out a cigarette and tapped its end downwards on the lid of the box. Then, rolling his tongue across his lips, he put it in his mouth. He tried to light up using his lighter, but the wind kept blowing it out. He hunched over, making a cave of his overcoat to provide shelter, and lit his fag as his head was buried within it. I noticed the nicotine stains on his fingers. Instead of turning to me with one of his army tales, he sat staring out across the countryside, not seeing but staring. I wasn't quite expecting what came next.

'There are some things you can't forget. You want to but they won't go away… this was fifteen years ago to the day… I killed a man. As a soldier, you must kill a lot of people, but mostly they are well out of sight, and you've no idea whether you've hit anyone. This time I came across this German soldier and took him by surprise. He was only about ten yards away; close enough to see his features… he had a birthmark, one of those red patches, you know, on his left temple. For a split second it reminded me of a man in our village, Benjamin Powell, though Benjamin didn't have a birthmark. But their build, their complexion, were just the same. I could have been mistaken, of course, I only had a split second. He began to raise his gun towards me… and I shot him. The bullet hit him in the face and the birthmark disappeared in a splash of blood. I didn't mean to hit him there, but you have to act quickly or you're a goner. It was him or me. It was what we were trained for. He fell to the ground screaming, but he wasn't dead. I shot him again, in the head, to finish him off. He went quiet. It was what soldiers were doing all over Europe. But it was *me* that did this. Some of my mates said they would frisk the body of anyone they killed to look for souvenirs they called them. One chap got a gold wristwatch. I couldn't touch this man, not even to check if he was dead. I've got lots of war memories, and most of them are good to recall. But this one was awful, and I don't want to remember it… but it won't go away. It's as though it's permanently fixed in my brain and won't fade away. Ever.'

I'd never heard Dad say so much, and I didn't know how to respond. I was only ten, but I understood enough to know that this was not a conversation. My role was like a priest hearing confession.

Throughout this he was drawing on his cigarette. I said nothing, but I was upset. Here was my hero, and now I was seeing him, not as the strong man I'd always seen but a beaten man weighed down. I thought I saw tears in his eyes, but it could have been the smoke from his cigarette or the late autumn wind blowing across the moor.

'When I came back, I was scared of meeting Benjamin. He was a local lad and we'd been to school together, but not in the same class. I imagined going into the Legion and coming up close to him. But it didn't happen; it couldn't happen. He didn't come back from the war. Fortunately for me, I suppose, but not for him. Not for him. But this German chap is still there in my head.'

He stubbed out his cigarette and put the dog-end in his tobacco tin. 'Come on, let's go home. Mam will be wondering where we are.'

It was the last time he took me up there. It must have been the autumn of 1952. The king had died earlier in the year, and the queen was to be crowned the following year. It was as though the country was pivoting away from a grey past to a more hopeful future. I couldn't see that at the time, but if you read about that period the same story is told. I was turning too, as I was moving from primary to secondary school, from childhood to adolescence. I was getting older and heavier and a greater strain on his legs. We wouldn't have gone up there in the winter anyway, and when the spring came, I wanted to go with my mates. But I remembered that day, that date, and it became an anniversary for me too. On that day, he ceased to be the all-conquering, all-knowing idol and became human. In later years, when I understood the meaning of that day, I would notice my dad spending more time than usual at his little bower at the end of the garden on the anniversary. He carried that bruising memory around with him for the next thirty years, but it had gone with him now.

We used to go up there when we were teenagers, sometimes on our bikes, straining our developing muscles to defy gravity. That was after Billy died; he would never have made it to the top, and we wouldn't have left him behind, so we didn't come.

The cottage on the hill was a tantalising prospect, but its state of disrepair and the intrusion of nature with its nettles and thorns overcame our curiosity. We speculated on its long-gone inhabitants, a wizard perhaps, an old soldier, a wolves' lair. That it might be just a poor shepherd and his family didn't seem to be exciting enough. Gordon tried to get inside it once but soon came stumbling back when some animal ran from the thick grass across his path, a rat perhaps, but bigger in his eyes. Thereafter we gave it no more than a suspicious glance as we sped by to safer activities.

Now, I walked to the end of the parapet. I looked up to the bend in the road and wondered if the primroses would be blooming near the top, hoping they might be, but knowing it was too early in the year. Anyway, it was getting towards evening, and I hadn't the will to go further. To my left, there was a rough path down to the track cut into the banking. It allowed walkers access to the trail even though it was now crossed by branches of hazel, their nuts ripening in their only autumn. I thought about going down, to stand on the track, to confront the memory. But I had had enough of confronting memories that day. But, like Dad, I had a bruising memory fixed inside me. It was Billy being hit by the train. And it wouldn't go away. It never appeared in my dreams that I knew of; it only emerged in daytime to disturb my peace of mind. Anyway, even if I got down to the track, I wasn't convinced I could get up again. I was tired. Life had become too complicated. It was OK on the road. Out, selling. New people every day. No need for friendship, no need for trust beyond the needs of a sale. No need for loyalty except to myself, and I'm easy to please. But, suddenly, people I cared about would not let me rest.

Rest in peace, Billy.
I needed a drink.

★★★

On the way back I stopped at a gate leading into the field between the railway line and Burton's Farm. About thirty yards into the field was a big sign staked into the ground. I was surprised I hadn't noticed it before; it must have been masked by the mature roadside trees – saplings when I last came.

> Manor Meadows
> Prestige development of
> three- and four-bedroom
> detached houses.
> Freehold

There was a telephone number for some company in Cooksley.

But beyond the sign, towards the middle of the field, something had changed. There used to be a big oak tree in the middle of the field. We used to climb as near to the top as we could. We did that after Billy died and we didn't want to go home. That's what trees are for, climbing, aren't they? And from its branches we could look down on the pond below. Unlike the stream by the church, the pond was not to be paddled in, its depths dark and sinister; weeds and slime threatening safety, its very stillness a deterrent. Nevertheless, we played at its edges, funnelled frogspawn into jam jars which we took home, intending to replicate the pond in our gardens but usually letting the eggs dry out to death in some corner. Gary reckoned he knew the difference between frogspawn and toadspawn, but he was never convincing. We did once catch a newt but, in a rare spirit of generosity, threw it back in. Frogs mated without inhibition before our eyes, though at first we thought them only giving each other piggy backs. As we realised we were watching sex at first hand, schoolboy embarrassment crept in. We watched the water boatmen glide into the middle of the pond beyond our reach. Dragonflies fluttered tantalisingly over the surface. Even in winter it held our fascination. After one very cold night, we were delighted to find the pond frozen over and dared each other to skate on it; none did. A branch thrown into the middle of the pond to break the ice and gradually slip below the surface was enough of a deterrent. When the snow came, we made a big snowball, pushing it around the field until it was taller than us and then finally letting it roll down the sloping bank of the pond until it slid slowly towards the middle and disappeared under the ice. But why all that effort to have it disappear? Fun, of course, fun.

But they weren't there – no tree, no pond. The field was featureless. What was going on here?

★★★

The Anchor had just opened its doors. I was its first customer. That pleased me. I wanted to be alone, but soon Howard came in. We sat at the bar and I bought him a drink.

'Sorry about your father.'

'Ta. Mam says can you come to the funeral? Friday, two-thirty. Something to eat at the community hall afterwards.'

'Yes. I'd be pleased to do that. I expect it was a bit of a shock.'

'It was expected, wasn't it?'

'It's expected for all of us.' Howard was uneasily jolly.

'Did Billy expect it?' Why the fuck did I say that?

Howard looked at me, silent for a while.

'No, he didn't. But what's that got to do with your father?'

I didn't know. I didn't think it did, but I hadn't got control of the connections.

'Tell me, Howard. Who shouted at Billy to cross the line?'

'We all did.'

'But who did it last – before he died?'

Howard looked uncomfortable. 'I think you did.'

No, I didn't. It wasn't me. It was Gordon.

'Billy was such a little kid. Younger than us but smaller too. And that leg.'

'It was a long time ago, Peter. There's no point in raking up the past. We were kids.'

'When do we stop being kids, Howard? When?'

Neither of us had an answer, and after a pause when we both sipped our drinks, I remembered the pond and the tree when we were kids. I continued, 'And another thing, Howard, what's happening up on Burton's field, the tree, the pond, they've gone. What's all that Manor Meadows stuff?'

Howard sipped his drink again, as did I, awaiting an explanation.

'How long have you got?'

'As long as it takes, mate. As long as it takes.'

'I told you on Sunday my father was well off and, like many rich men, he wanted to be even richer. It's understandable in his case. His father was a poor tenant farmer, and he helped my father buy his first farm.'

'*First* farm!'

'In later years he bought up several other farms as local farmers lost the appetite to work the long hours needed – or at least their sons did. One of the farms he bought was from Josiah Burton. The farm buildings were converted for residential use and Father sold them on. Did quite well.'

'But why more building on the field? It's ruining this village. It's greedy.'

'Let me ask you a question. I assume you've got a nice house. Modern, I guess.'

I nodded.

'Wasn't it built on a field? What did it destroy? Who played on that? Are there hedges around the estate? Is there a nice tree in the middle? And those houses where your mother and father live, what was there before they were built? And the council estate beyond?'

He'd got me there, but I persisted. 'But we used to play in that field – the five of us. I mean six. It was where we spent our childhood.'

'And you wanted to get away. This place wasn't good enough for you. And I suppose you wanted this place to stay unchanged just so you could be comforted when you came back. If you lived here, like me and Bendy and Gary, we would have had to stagnate so you could feel superior.'

He was right, of course, but I couldn't let go. 'What about Manor Meadows?'

'One thing you learn in business is not to overreach yourself. I tried to explain the tax situation to my father, but he was too stubborn to listen. He owed a lot and needed cash. To get some capital, he decided to sell some land for housing. The field where we used to play had been designated Green Belt, but somehow he managed to get it reclassified when he did up the farm buildings.'

'How did he manage that?'

'I'd rather not say, but I had no say over it. He was still in charge.'

'And then what?'

'Well, Father judged he would get a better price for the land if it was free of the pond and the tree. The tree was an oak and protected of course, and he did have plans to cut it down, hoping nobody would notice. Fortunately, it fell down during one of the big storms a few years ago. We sold the trunk and the big branches to Bennetts and the off-cuts to The Manor for firewood. So that problem was solved.'

Bennetts! Dad might have used that wood for his coffin. He was being buried in my playground.

'But the pond, that would still be there.'

Howard looked uncomfortable. 'Hang on a minute. I'm just going to the toilet.'

I looked around the bar. An old guy on the far wall nodded to me and said, 'Sorry to hear about your dad. He was a good bloke. I knew him a long time.'

Did he know about Auntie Pauline? Did he help the rumours spread? I couldn't trust anybody now.

'I'm sorry, I don't remember you.'

'Albert Percival. I used to have the grocers opposite the church.'

I remembered him then, though I didn't know his first name. Percival was the name above the shop.

'Do you still have the shop?'

'No. I couldn't compete with the little supermarket in the precinct. I was too old to start again.'

'Do you come in here much?'

'No. I usually go to the Legion. That's where I used to meet your dad.'

'Well, the funeral's on Friday at two-thirty. A bit to eat in the community hall afterwards. I'm sure Dad would have liked that.'

'There's a notice up in the Legion. Nice black surround. Very tasteful.'

Howard was emerging from the toilets at the back.

'Ta-ta now, nice to see you again. See you Friday perhaps... in the hall,' I said to Dad's friend, as he was now in my eyes.

When Howard came back, he picked up his glass and guided us to the corner seats near the door. Howard sat down next to me, sitting uneasily, and said, 'It's more private here. Less likely to be overheard.'

After we'd both taken a drink, I said, 'The pond?'

'The pond... look, I don't want others to know this. You know how rumours spread.'

Oh yes, I know how rumours spread, Howard.

Howard glanced at Mr Percival and some other drinkers further down the bar. He drew his face closer to mine. 'Father, not me you understand, had the idea of filling in the pond. He'd noticed that when he'd sold the farm buildings there was no record in the maps of a pond in that field, so as far as the authorities were concerned, it didn't exist. First, he drained the pond, pumping the water to the railway embankment, hoping the drainage there would take it away.'

'Hoping! It was a lot of water.'

Howard shrugged. 'Well, it worked. We cleared the banks of branches and saplings, burned them and put the residue in where the pond had been. Then he took loads of stones we had at the quarry and toppled them in. Then he covered them up with a couple of feet of top soil and some turves from another field. A couple of hours with the heavy roller and it was done. So that when we sold it to a builder, he had a nice flat field to build on.'

'Wasn't that a bit underhand, Howard? The builder could have built a house – a prestige house – on top of a landfill. Never mind underhand, it would be dangerous, wouldn't it?'

'Yes. But father knew the builder, and they agreed no houses would be built on that spot. In fact, it makes a nice little roundabout. The plans are in the council offices.'

'So that's all right is it, Howard?' I said, with my voice rising.

'Shush.'

'What about all those little creatures in there crushed by your fucking stones? What about the countryside and your fucking houses ruining it?'

I could see Howard bridling, which was unusual. He brought his face closer to mine.

'Aren't you being a bit of a hypocrite? I don't think you cared all that much for the wildlife. Who was it that took frogs and put them on the railway track to see them squashed by a train? Who was it that took a pellet gun to the birds in your beloved tree? Who fired a catapult at Mrs Henshaw's dog? Who threw firecrackers among the hens in Burton's yard? Who boasted the biggest collection of birds eggs in the village?'

'We all did.'

'Yes, we all did that when we were a gang of kids together thirty years ago. I think what upsets you about us filling in the pond is that it filled in a patch in your memory, and now it's gone. It was your childhood and it's been taken from you.'

'But it was your childhood too.'

'Yes, it was, and I enjoyed it too, but it doesn't dominate my life.'

He was right of course, but he had his nice settled daily life, his wealth, his future, and what had I got? I was getting emotional, not quite crying but filling up. I stood up to get at the hanky from my trouser pocket to blow my nose. I was losing it; it was time to go home.

Go home. What home?

'I'm sorry, Howard. It's an emotional time. I hadn't realised how emotional all this had made me.'

'Well, don't forget. I lost my father too, although he didn't linger. Nevertheless, he left me with baggage as well. But let's not go into that now.'

'No. Let's not.'

'You're a bit upset, Peter. Let me run you home. Your mother could do with the company.'

She didn't need me. She had Freda next door. And Mr Baverstock. And the whole of Africa. She'd be all right. She had things. What had I got?

'No. Thanks. I'm OK. It's been more upsetting than I thought. I'll get some air on the way home. See you on Friday at the funeral. Cheers.'

'Want another, Howard?' called the barman as I was leaving.

Howard looked up from his glass.

'Just a half, George. Then I'll get off home.'

I was glad I hadn't had another pint. For one thing I'd have been home later, and the food was already drying out in the oven when I got in.

'Sorry, Mam. I went for a walk. Took longer than I thought. Not as young as I was.' Almost not a lie.

'You've been to the pub. I can smell your breath.' She was unusually accusing.

'Just stopped in for a quick half.' Only half a lie there. 'Howard sends his best wishes. His sympathies I mean.'

'Did you invite him to the funeral? I'd like him to come. He was always polite to Dad.'

Everyone was friendly with Dad. He didn't have an enemy in the world. Was I his enemy now?

'Did you invite Pauline?'

'Yes. She'll be there.'

I couldn't understand why Mam wanted to ask her.

'That'll be nice. Dad would have liked that.'

'What about you, Mam? Is that what you'd like?'

'What I like isn't the point. It's Dad's funeral, and I want anyone who's been close to him there.'

'Whatever you say.'

She was so closed. I really didn't know what she was thinking. Yet she was pure and simple and nice and honest and religious. She couldn't be that forgiving. Did she know there was something to forgive?

WEDNESDAY

'Mr Worsley phoned.'

I dropped a piece of bacon off my fork, splashing my shirt front with fat. Head office. Ken Worsley. What did he want? 'When did he ring?'

'While you were out yesterday. I forgot all about it until I saw the pad just now. Mr Kenneth Worsley. I've put his number on the pad.'

I knew the number. It was tattooed on my brain.

'What did he say?'

'Just asked you to ring as soon as you could. Seemed a nice man. Very polite.'

Nice! Worsley! I wouldn't trust him as far as I could throw him. I looked at my watch. Quarter to nine. He'd be in the office now. I gobbled down the bacon and eggs as fast as I could and slurped a mouthful of tea.

'Peter, you'll get indigestion eating like that.'

If that was all I got, I'd be content.

'Ken. Peter Carter here. Sorry I didn't get back earlier. Only just got your message. What can I do for you?'

'How are things with you, Peter? Any developments?'

'My father died two days ago. The funeral's on Friday.'

'Peter. I'm so sorry. I hope it wasn't too distressing.'

Not for me. I couldn't speak for Dad.

'No. He went quietly in the end. For the best really.'

'These things happen. Is your mother all right?'

Why didn't he get to the point?

'She's taking it very well. It was expected.'

'They'd been married a long time I suppose.'

This wasn't going to be good news.

'Yes. Nearly fifty years.'

'Fifty! My, my… so, when can we expect you back?'

'I'm staying until Sunday. Just to get my mother settled. I was planning to be back in the office on Monday.'

'Good. Yes. That would be helpful. We've got some things to talk about.'

'Concerning me?'

'Yes, in a way. We're changing the direction of the company. We may have a new role for you.'

May have!

'Sounds interesting.'

'I don't want to go into detail now. Too big an issue. See you Monday then. Can you make it first thing? And, Peter, can you bring the company car keys and documentation with you? Your new role could be office-based so you won't need transport.'

But how was I going to get about? Maureen would need her car. How would I get to the office? Same bus I get now, I expect.

'Yes. OK, Ken. Understood. I'll be there. Thanks for ringing.'

'My pleasure. Goodbye, Peter.'

Goodbye, Peter. Shit.

'Goodbye, Ken.'

I put the phone down. What was that all about? They couldn't be going to get rid of me. Could they? I'd been their top salesman for years now. But you never knew with these head office people. Look how they got rid of Andy Martindale last year. Poor sod had a small heart attack and next thing you know: goodbye, Mr Martindale.

I sat down at the table again.

'Are you all right, Peter? You look a bit pale.'

'Rushing my food, I expect. Just something cropped up at work. Nothing to worry about.'

Nothing? A top salesman's no good if he can't get out on the road. When was my licence due back? March, April, May. Christ, that was months yet. Half a year. More. Oh shit.

'Would you like another cup?'

'Yes. Thanks.'

'What are you going to do today?'

'I don't know.' But I did. 'I might go out after dinner. Just for a pint and a walk.'

'You're doing quite a lot of walking these days, Peter.'

'Yeah.' And drinking.

★★★

Sally was there. Just where I'd first seen her. Her glass was nearly full.

'Hi.'

'Hello, Peter. I'm sorry about your dad.'

'Thanks. How'd you hear?'

'Howard.'

'Of course.'

'Is your mother OK?'

She'd never met her. Why did she want to know?

'Yeah. She's OK. Pint of that, please, and a packet of fags. Those.'

The young barman put the pint on the bar and took the fiver. I looked across at Sally, then down at her glass and asked with my eyes.

'No. Not for me, thanks. I only want the one.'

The barman put the change on the bar and moved to the other end. I didn't know what to say. But she kept the conversation flowing.

'When's the funeral?'

'Friday.'

'At the churchyard?'

'Yes.'

'He's not being cremated?'

I wanted to tell her about the coffin. About the craftsmanship. I wanted to tell her about his hands covering mine as he guided the plane all those years ago. Hands now lacking that firm grip. Sinewy hands that had made the box in which they now lay. Dead hands holding nothing. She wouldn't want to know.

'No.'

'Your family are coming over, aren't they?'

Why did she want to know? I supposed she was going to turn up. Just to see.

'Yeah. Coming over tomorrow and staying until Saturday.'

'I know – I saw her booking in the diary this morning.'

'Oh.'

She must have sensed my alarm. 'Don't worry, I won't be seeing them. I'm off duty for a couple of days. I've put them in good rooms.'

'Thanks.' And was I relieved.

'Are you going back with them?'

'No, I'm staying 'til Sunday.'

How much more did she want to know? But I was glad she was talking. About nothing really. But talking and taking my mind off things.

'Well, I must go now.'

I didn't want her to leave me.

'Are you sure you won't have another?'

'No, really. I do this too often. Putting on a bit of weight.'

I glanced at her body, and below the bulge of her breasts, her stomach rode above the tight waistband of her black skirt. I wanted to draw my hand over its comforting fleshiness.

'Can I walk back with you?'

She gave me an old-fashioned look. 'OK, but no more.'

'No, honestly.' I drained my glass.

I stood looking through her kitchen window as she filled the kettle. It was her suggestion I came in for coffee, but there was no hint of anything more in her voice. I felt she was mothering me, and I was comforted enough by that. Beyond her small garden was the hedge of leylandii masking Auntie Pauline's garden. I thought I detected a movement. Was it her or just her washing on the line? Was she looking for flowers for the grave – or just remembering? Remembering what? There wouldn't be many blooms now. Better to buy some. Or was it important they were from her garden?

'Let's sit in the front.'

'How do you spend your time at home?'

'TV. Books and magazines from work.'

'Men friends?'

'Mind your own business.'

With some women you'd take that as a yes, but with her I couldn't be sure.

'Do you think about your hubby?'

'Yes. A lot.'

'What's he in for?' I asked, hoping she wouldn't say GBH.

'Why do you want to know?'

I shrugged. 'It's not important.' But in its way, its little way, it was.

'Fraud. He had his own company, and he found ways of siphoning off clients' money into a private account.'

'And you didn't know?'

'No.'

'What did he do with the money?'

She took a sip of her coffee as though gathering her thoughts. 'We met when we were quite young. I worked for an estate agent. He came in looking for somewhere to rent and we just clicked. After a while he decided to set up his own company – something to do with loans and mortgages – and it did really well. I mean really, *really* well. Although, I kept working – for my independence, I suppose. We had a nice house – four bedrooms, two en suite, double garage, a cleaner and a gardener. All gone now. Holidays – Maldives, Barbados, Cape Town. Jewellery. I've still got most of that. Unless you're a policeman, in which case I haven't. So, we had the *good life*. Losing it was a bit of a blow.'

'Didn't you guess?'

'Not really. You don't believe the person you're so close to, the person you love, would do something like that.'

An image of Dad and Auntie Pauline flashed through my mind. 'I suppose not.'

'But he was doing it for the both of us. He just got out of his depth and couldn't confront the truth. I suspect at the end he was just waiting for the car crash, unable to do anything to stop it.'

'You said *love*. What do you mean by that?'

'It's shorthand for a lot of things and probably means different things to different people. I don't want to analyse it. I just feel it. Don't you?'

Served me right for asking.

'Any kids?'

'No. We kept putting it off.'

'It's not too late.'

She smiled. 'Time's passing by.'

Time.

'When's he due out?'

'About three years. Maybe less if he behaves.'

'It must have been a lot of money and a lot of people – victims… and you'll carry on where you left off?'

'I'd like to, yes.'

'You still love him after all that?' I shouldn't have asked. I didn't really want to know, but the conversation was flowing, with me making the running. I suddenly felt in control, she the vulnerable one.

'Yes.' Her voice was quiet but firm.

'Did you forgive him?'

'Forgive him? I didn't need to do that. He hadn't done anything to *me*.'

I wondered. He wouldn't be the same bloke. She wasn't the same person. She had stuck by him. Given up a lot. Why would she do it? Done without sex. So, she says. For love! Women!

'Women can do that, can't they?'

'What?'

'Stand by people. Make sacrifices.' I was thinking of Auntie Pauline. Not of Auntie Pauline and Dad, but Auntie Pauline and Harry and hoping that was true.

'And men can't?'

'No. Maybe they can, but they don't.'

'How sad.'

'I don't suppose that's a surprise to you.'

'No, but it's still sad. There's a woman up at The Manor. She's quite old now. Miss Smithers. She was going to be married. To a fighter pilot. But he was shot down in the war. She's lived on without him for forty years or so. Hasn't wanted anybody else in all that time, though she was quite good-looking in her day. She's got photos of the two of them in her room. And on the anniversary of his death, she doesn't leave her room. Has all her meals delivered. She had good looks, a good education, a bit of money and she's a really nice person. Could have had somebody else but chose not to.'

'Why?'

'That word again. Love, I suppose.'

Fucking ridiculous.

'How do you know all this?'

'We've talked about it.'

'As women do?'

'As women do. As women can.'

'What makes you think men don't talk about things to each other. Personal things.'

'Do they? Do *you*?' Suddenly, she was in charge.

I shook my head slowly. 'But this woman put herself above temptation, didn't she. Locked herself away from the world in your hotel. Wasn't close to another man. But suppose. Just suppose she lived in her own house. Went out to work maybe. Worked closely with another man. He might have made an approach. She'd have to choose then. A real choice. Do you think she'd have chosen loyalty then? Do you?' I could feel the defensive belligerence in my voice.

'I think you're presuming to know this woman. You've got her nicely pigeonholed into one of your male boxes.'

'Maybe. But I still think that a man and a woman who are close together for long periods of time are going to want to fuck each other. Will fuck each other. Won't they? Go on, admit it.'

'Do you mean your dad and Mrs Dobson?'

It knocked the wind out of me. I knew I was thinking about them, but I didn't think *she* was. I didn't think she knew. I shot to my feet. I didn't know what to say. I stumbled to the door and walked away.

★★★

I paused at the top of Sally's road, taking stock. Auntie Pauline's house was just fifty yards down the road. She would be in there alone. Did she deserve that? OK, she and Dad were lovers, but it didn't affect me until then. And I didn't know if it was true even now. It could have been all innocent. If it was true, could I forgive her, forgive Dad? That's a big ask. If she was innocent and wanted to put flowers on his grave just through gratitude and nothing more, shouldn't I do it for her? I turned towards her front door.

'Hello, Peter. You're back again. Come in.'

I didn't want a long discussion in case some truth came out; I could just about cope with the half-truths. 'I wondered whether there were any flowers in the garden I could put by the coffin.'

She paused, and I waited. 'That's a nice idea. I'd like that. Let's go and see what we can find.'

There was a path down one edge of the garden alongside the leylandii. It led to a small greenhouse which I hadn't seen before. Auntie Pauline struggled to open the door as there seemed some problem with the latch.

'Eric would have mended that, but it's a bit much for me.'

I eased her to one side and repaired the latch. Inside was a collection of pots. Some contained plants

I recognised as chrysanthemums. The sturdier of the display was a bronze colour. I looked around for something to cut them with. There were some secateurs attached to a strut in the frame by a cup hook. Well done, Dad.

I cut five of them. One for Dad... one for Mam... one for me... one for Harry... and one for Auntie Pauline.

We returned to the house uncomfortably quiet.

'They don't need wrapping. I'll see they get there.'

I went down her front steps and turned to say goodbye. I didn't say anything as I feared I might cry. I just raised the blooms in her direction and offered a smile.

Instead of going down the main road, I struck off across the playing fields, down the council estate road, past Dad's old works and went into the undertaker's office.

Mr Stevens got up from his chair. 'What have we got here, Mr Carter?'

Well, it was obvious, wasn't it?

'Can these be put with Dad's coffin?'

'Of course. I'll put them in some water until Friday. Would you like them tied up?'

'Could you put four of them in a bunch on top and one inside before you screw it down?'

One inside? Who was that from? Me... Mam... or Auntie Pauline?

THURSDAY

I was in the back room watching the snooker. Mam was in the kitchen.

'They're here.' Mam announced the arrival of Maureen and the kids.

'Hello.'

'Hello, Maureen love. Did you have a good journey? Aren't the roads awful these days?'

Mam didn't even drive. Their voices echoed in the kitchen. There was a silence, and I came across them hugging. Maureen looked at me over Mam's shoulders and, in smiling, squeezed tears from her eyes. I blinked.

'How are you?' Maureen said, this to Mam not me.

'I'm all right. Thanks.'

'And you, Peter. I'm so sorry. You've had a difficult two weeks.'

Well, it had been busy, that was for sure. I saw Claire passing the kitchen window and then the stooped figure of William. He'd got a Mohican haircut. Jesus.

I looked at Maureen and nodded just before she hugged me too. She held me close and there was no doubt about her sincerity. I felt myself filling up and my chest heaving against her. No crying. Not in front of the kids. Not in front of anyone really. I eased Maureen away. She might have thought it was a push. It wasn't. It really wasn't.

'Hi, Dad.' Claire hugged me too and I felt her growing womanliness. I eased her away, too scared of what I felt.

William did not hug me. He just stood in front of me, looking guilty. I realised how much taller he was than me. His haircut made him look even taller. I didn't know what to say or what to do. Hug him. No way. Shake his hand. No. I squeezed his upper arm.

'Hello, William.'

'Hi.'

I didn't know how he felt. He was a stranger. It shouldn't be like that. Not father and son. He was a difficult so-and-so.

'Come through.' We were all stood in the small kitchen like passengers in a lift, physically closer than we'd have wished, the nearness breeding formality. Mam led the way to the back room.

We had a light dinner. Mam had made some sandwiches. She had remembered Claire was vegetarian now.

A sponge cake to follow. Was that all she could bake? I never saw anything different. She always took one to the bring-and-buy at the church. Perhaps that's all she learnt at school. She left at fourteen so didn't have time to learn much. She did have a go at Christmas pudding one year, but it wasn't a great success, and she relied on the church sales after that. We had a cup of tea, and Mam invited us into the front room. The front room!

William stayed in the back room – for the snooker. Mam asked how the kids were doing. Claire had her GCSEs next summer and William – well, what would he be doing? He said he wanted to be a furniture designer – that week anyway. To design it, not to build it, mark you. Dad could have helped him there, except…

Mam blurted out about Ken Worsley phoning.

'It's no problem, don't worry.'

'You've got your annual company health check coming up on the first of next month don't forget,' said Maureen.

I had forgotten, but then I put it all together – loss of licence, increased car insurance, change of direction for the company, different role for me, loss of company car, health check, meeting Monday morning. There would be a lot of hurdles ahead. Shit.

Maureen and the kids had booked into The Manor, and about four o'clock, they decided to check in. Mam and I agreed to join them for an evening meal – a treat for Mam, an ordeal for me, a fear of Sally making an unexpected appearance.

★★★

Mam didn't want to eat late, so we arranged to meet at about six-thirty. We walked up and entered the grounds between two stone pillars with wrought-iron gates pegged open. From there, we could see the frontage of the old building, with a modern residential block down one side and a large plastic-framed dining area on the other. Through the glass we could see staff serving the few early diners. We stepped from the gravelled approach through two heavy wooden doors and a pair of reinforced glass ones behind.

Mam would have known the layout inside from working there a lifetime ago. I couldn't even guess what she made of it now.

I glanced apprehensively at the check-in desk, even though Sally had said she would be off duty. There was no one behind the counter, but when we stood in the foyer, a slim Asian man came hurrying forwards. We asked for the Borthwick Bar and, after indicating where it was, he took our coats to a room beyond the reception desk.

I found Maureen and the kids sitting with drinks in front of them. I wanted a beer, and Mam decided she'd like a sherry. Mam never drank alcohol. What would she come out with? I knew how alcohol loosened the tongue.

Throughout the meal, Claire was in deep conversation with Mam. It was nice to watch; a couple two generations apart talking as though they were friends. She wanted to know what Mam could remember of working here.

'Well, we were downstairs mainly. We had some duties up here. Cleaning and polishing and laying the fires. Sometimes of an evening, for special occasions, we came up to help if the owners had a lot of dinner guests. We used to take their coats and hats. Lovely material a lot of it was. Pauline and I used to drape the clothes over our arms and store them away in a little room just off the lobby. Where they put our coats just now. And when the guests were eating, Pauline and I used to try on some of the topcoats. Lucky we didn't get caught, else we'd have been sacked. There were a surprising number of top hats; you don't see many now. Mainly funerals. The lobby out there smells different now. Back then it used to smell of polish. Hardly surprising when you think how long Pauline and I spent rubbing the woodwork. It smells a bit too clean now, like a doctor's waiting room. This room was the dining room then, so that hasn't changed. Only the food I expect. There was a lot of food left over, and when we'd finished our shift, we would go down to the kitchen to find something tasty for ourselves.'

Claire seemed to lap all this up as though she was interested. Perhaps she was. 'Did you enjoy the work you did?'

'Enjoy? I don't suppose we thought of that. We had jobs; that seemed enough. There wasn't much choice unless you wanted to milk cows.'

Throughout this conversation, Maureen and I sat next to each other, listening but not talking much. I felt her hand reach out for mine below the tablecloth. Whenever Claire asked a question, Maureen squeezed my hand. We both felt pride, I think. It was a good feeling.

From where I was sitting, I could see the reception desk, and I couldn't stop glancing that way until Maureen had brought my attention back to the table. We had a two-course meal, but William wanted a sweet. It's amazing how much people can put away when they're not paying. When it came to settle up, I offered my credit card to the waiter, who came back a few minutes later and whispered in my ear that it had been refused. But it was the company card. And it had been refused!

Maureen came to the rescue with cash, but nevertheless it was another indicator of where things were going with my job.

It was a risky journey home with neither of us totally sober, but Mam and me made it safely in the end. As we approached the house, I could see the upstairs bedroom curtains were closed and the light behind them lit. I knew there was no one there and Mam would have known too. I opened the front door – too dark to go round the back at this time of night. As the hall light fell across her face, I could see Mam's eyes behind her glasses, usually calm, now moist and blinking.

If we had to drink alcohol to show emotion, then here's to it.

FRIDAY

So much happened that day – the day of the funeral. I don't believe some of it even now. I woke to the sun shining on the bedroom curtains. It had done so many years ago. Same sun; same curtains, I expect, bought to last. I went to the bathroom and opened the frosted-glass window. I looked over the garden to the bower at the end where Dad and me had sat and chatted, like mates I'd like to think, but we were never equal. He was Dad. And he'd chosen a good day to be buried. Bright sunshine, clear sky. Just like we looked forward to on our holidays. A day to die for.

I couldn't escape him – not that I wanted to – even in the bathroom. The wooden panel hiding the bath, the cupboard containing the emersion heater, the shelving for glasses and brushes, the pelmet over the window, all showed his hand. I closed the window to shut out the cool autumn air. I shaved, and the mirror reflected a face older by more than the two weeks I'd spent there.

The hearse arrived, and we filed out to gather behind it, as we were walking the few hundred yards to the church. I looked around to see we were all there. William, with that haircut, looked like a plumed horse; he should have been at the front pulling.

Maureen had brought my black coat and suit and a clean white shirt. I hadn't a tie to wear, but I wore one of Dad's. It felt good wearing it. I walked with Mam, and Maureen came behind with the kids. But there were others behind her. People I didn't know but who seemed to know me nodded sympathetically. I probably had known most of them, but they had been forgotten in the ferment of my later life. As we walked, our view was dominated by the black frame of the hearse, but I could see the fine, polished coffin, with its brass plate covered by the single bunch of flowers from Auntie Pauline's garden. As I glanced to the side, I could see small groups of people gathered at garden gates. Men with bare heads, children unusually still. At the time, I thought they must have been honouring Dad, but I guess many of them were remembering a loss of their own, other parents, spouses, children even, and our funeral was only the excuse for this. No matter, we were all sharing that day. There weren't that many, but I hadn't expected any. I'd like Dad to have seen them, but he couldn't see.

It wasn't very far to the church, but it seemed ages. I could see the chrysanthemums on the top of the coffin just covering the name plate. I wondered, did any of the watching neighbours count them and wonder why there were four? Which of them knew the rumour about Dad and Auntie Pauline? How many believed it? Would any of them have changed the view when they saw four flowers? I suppose I thought that those things, weighing heavily on my mind, occupied their waking day too. How ridiculous. I had to believe that the fifth bloom was inside the coffin, clasped in Dad's hands perhaps. You have to trust an undertaker, don't you?

I held my mother's hand. But really, she held mine like those holidays so long ago. Just keeping me from harm. Not wanting me to stray. But I had strayed. Not then but since. We paused at the church gates while the ushers unloaded the coffin. They paused to steady their load before setting off up the path and in front of us. The coffin was good, solid stuff. Just like Dad used to be. Not like he was then, now he was balsa wood not oak. Halfway up the path to the church door, the ushers stopped. I looked at Mam, not knowing what was happening.

'We're just pausing by his parents' grave. He wanted that.'

His parents, long gone. I scanned the headstone for a name. There it was. Alfred Carter. Alfred. I never knew that. From the date I could see he died before I was born. And his wife Annie died after I was born, but I don't remember her. The pall-bearers paused to let the mourners go into the church. The procession moved on before I could weigh things up. At the church door, the vicar was waiting to receive us. Flanking him, were two men – Dad's age. I recognised one of them as Albert Percival who I met in The Anchor. They both wore military berets and dark blazers with ribbons and medals. They held two regimental flags sloping at an upward angle. I was going to cry but held it in check. I wouldn't get a send-off like this. Why should I?

The church was full, and as the family went down the aisle, the congregation turned to face it. Mam stopped and looked around her. I saw her look to a pew on her side towards the back of the church. Auntie Pauline. Oh no! Mam turned back, easing William to one side, and walked over to Auntie Pauline. I didn't know what to expect. I didn't want a row. But there was no row. Mam took Auntie Pauline by the hand and led her to join me at the head of the procession. What the hell was Mam doing? The whole congregation was looking, I thought. They all knew about Auntie Pauline and Dad. Didn't they?

Mam ushered Auntie Pauline into the front pew. They sat down still holding hands. I took my place at the end next to the aisle. I picked up the order of service and there on the front cover was a photo of Dad, in his prime I suppose, not like the man I'd been close to for two weeks now.

As the organ struck up, I looked backwards down the aisle to see the pall-bearers steady themselves as they climbed up the church steps. The sentinels at the door had lowered their flags as the coffin passed between them. I was now facing the other mourners. All eyes were towards me. What were they thinking?

Many of the men were wearing rows of medals on well-worn black suits, both reflecting the sunlight through the stained-glass windows. There were more women than men, and they favoured dark coats and veiled hats. There was a uniformity about their dress which reflected the conformity of the lives that had kept them content. These clothes had been there before and had many more outings ahead of them. Did Dad know all these people? Why not? He'd lived here all his life and his parents before him. And how many more generations? I'd no idea. Didn't know, even though that was my own family.

The service began, and I didn't know how to behave, but I followed Mam's singing, praying, standing, anticipating the next move from the corner of my eye. And beyond Mam I could see Auntie Pauline. Not quite as a figure but as a presence. And I could feel a hundred eyes on my back.

Mr Baverstock gave the eulogy. He described Dad's early life before the war; I didn't know any of it. He then recalled the man I knew, confirming my opinions of him. Since Dad never went to church, I wondered where the information came from. It had to be Mam. And Auntie Pauline!

As we followed the coffin back down the aisle, the mourners were then looking directly at us – Mam, me… and Auntie Pauline. What did they see? What were they thinking?

Outside, the sky had clouded over, but didn't threaten rain.

The mourners walked down a side path and stood before an open grave at its edge. I looked into the grave, and my stomach contracted as the coffin was lowered in. The vicar handed Mam a trowel full of earth. She put Auntie Pauline's hand over hers and held it with her other. And together they sprinkled the damp, brown soil over the coffin. I could hear the earth hitting the wood; a small stone struck more sharply. Did Dad hear that?

As Mam and I went towards the main gate, Auntie Pauline dropped a little apart from us. Several people offered their condolences – mainly to Mam, but some to me. Howard's face was one of the few I recognised, and its familiarity was a relief. He was standing to one side of the gate just inside the churchyard, on one of the very old gravestones that were now laid flat to make a pathway between some of the newer graves. We paused to talk. He nodded to someone passing behind me, and I turned to see Auntie Pauline going into the street. He didn't want to come to the community hall, but he offered to run me to the station on Sunday.

'Do you fancy a drink before I go home?' The word *home* stuck in my throat.

'We could have a drink in Cooksley, before the train comes.'

'Good idea.'

'Before then? Well, you'll know where I'll be.'

I nodded, and we shook hands. It's not what we did as lads, shake hands, but we weren't lads anymore. There was something about the formality of the occasion that demanded it. But I was comforted to feel Howard's living hand even though he was wearing gloves.

Once outside the gate, I found myself facing Auntie Pauline. It was probably no more than civility which made me ask, 'Will you come back across the road?'

Auntie Pauline shook her head. 'No. No, but thank you. I want to go home. I want a little peace and quiet.'

She came to me, held my face in her hands and kissed me on the cheek. In front of all those people! Had those lips kissed Dad? I imagined her melting under his embrace. I imagined…

'Goodbye, Peter. Come and see me before you go. Your mother and I have something to tell you.'

What now? Was she going to confess?

The community hall was across the road from the church. I remembered it being built, Dad and other men sawing, hammering, bricklaying, glazing. I recalled me and the other boys pushing wheelbarrows and stacking bricks. And, on one occasion, me and Gordon carrying long beams, one of us at each end. I looked up at the roof. They were still there. I wondered which one we carried. There were several, I think. It's a blur now.

I was looking up, waiting for the guests to follow from the church. The trestle tables were set out as they had been for weddings and wakes, fun and funerals, for nearly forty years. Maybe the women who stood behind them now – removing the Cellophane from the plates of sandwiches, turning the knob down on the steaming urn – had done that too for all those years. Perhaps they had always looked as they do now – middle aged, old even, and content. Or was it resignation? Acceptance? Mam was nearest the door and Maureen close behind and to my left. As we moved, I could feel her body touch mine, and it felt good she was there.

'Hello, Peter. How are you feeling?' It was one of the ladies behind the tables. Who was she?

What should I say? She knew me. 'Not so bad, you know.'

'Nice to see the family. They're looking well.'

Should I ask about hers? Supposing she didn't have one. 'And yours?' That was safe enough.

'Well, Walter's dead now, of course.' She said it so naturally.

'I'm sorry.'

'I'm a grandma now.'

'What of? I mean boy or girl.'

'A girl. Miranda. Helen's first. I don't think Gwen will have any.'

Helen? Helen and Gwen…? Mottershead! Yes, I remembered. Helen was a lot younger than me. Barely a teenager when I left home.

'Well, give her my regards.'

I could see Mam chatting with William who'd been lurking in the background. If I didn't know him, I'd have said he was laughing. Maureen came up to me. 'You OK?'

'Yeah. No point in not being, is there.'

'You'll miss Dad, won't you?'

'Why do you say that?'

'I never heard you speak ill of him, that's all. I liked him a lot. He was dead straight. No side to him. Your mum will miss him.'

'She's got all this lot.' I turned my eyes around the room, drawing in the small groups of mainly women, chatting, balancing cups of tea and plates of sandwiches. And what had I got?

'Yes. She'll be all right. And it looks as though she's made it up with Auntie Pauline.'

'What do you mean?'

'Your mam and Auntie Pauline? Well, it's a long story, isn't it?'

Was it? What did she know? 'I don't know. You tell me.'

'If your mam hasn't told you, you can't expect me to.'

'You mean you and Mam talked about it.'

'Of course. People need to talk about things.'

Women do! I took a bite of pie and bit my tongue. 'Ow.'

'Careful. What time are you coming back on Sunday?'

'I'm leaving here about four o'clock. Train gets in at five-forty. I'll ring you on Sunday morning to confirm.'

'I'll pick you up.'

'Ta. I've got to go into the office on Monday. Ken Worsley wants to talk to me. About the future. My future. I've got to take the car keys in and leave them. I won't have use of the car anymore.'

'Oh.'

'What do you mean by that? What do you know?'

'Nothing. But the way you said it made it sound as though there was a problem.' Women! Can they read minds?

'I don't know. I just don't know.'

SATURDAY

Maureen called in on her way home after checking out at The Manor. She took my two suitcases with my dirty washing, promising to have everything washed and ironed by Monday. She always washed my working clothes as soon as I got home from each trip. I wondered, did she smell them, and if she did, what could she sense on them? Women have a good nose for perfume.

Mam gave the kids some money – pocket money she called it. It was a note, but perhaps only a fiver. Still, a fiver was quite a lot for her.

When they had gone, I thought I would go to the cemetery to pay my last respects. I stood for a while at the gate looking over the gravestones – flat slabs and towers, marble and granite, grey and black, angels and birds, as varied as the lives of the people beneath them. They spread as far as the hedges and walls defining the graveyard, and the number and concentration of plots seemed to confirm the inevitability of death. There could be more people lying dead in here than are living in Eldon now. I had come back to Eldon expecting to be reconnected with the living, but looking over the stones, I seemed to be more connected to the dead. Confining people to this walled plot seemed to cut them off from the life they had shared. Cremation even more so, I supposed. I wondered if it was legal to bury a relative in your own back garden, front garden if you wanted, to make a point. I considered where I wanted to end up, the ground or the furnace. Deciding – hoping – it wasn't an imminent choice. I moved in among the gravestones.

I wanted to leave Dad's until the end so wandered between the plots. I suppose I wanted to see if I recognised any of the names. I came to the one I was trying to avoid, yet knowing it was there. Was I drawn to it?

William (Billy) Barker
2 November 1944–5 August 1953
Died in an accident

Billy. Oh, Billy. An accident! Was it? It was thirty years ago, and *he* can't remember it. But I do. It won't go away. And we caused it. We – his mates. We were older than him and supposed to look after him. But we didn't. We even caused his death, didn't we? Coaxed him over the line.

Come on. Come on, Billy. Quick.

We all said it, didn't we? We're all to blame, aren't we? But somebody shouted last. Somebody called out the last words he heard. I said it was Gordon, but Howard said it was me.

Sorry, Billy.

I wondered why his parents' names weren't listed as well, until I remembered they left the village a couple of years afterwards. Not wanting to be reminded I supposed, but perhaps just the pull of another job. Their names would be on another stone, their bodies in another soil, not with the remains of their only son. Yet I had gone out of my way to find him as though, in remembering, I had attached myself to him; reattached I supposed. I left Billy, wherever he was, in peace, I hoped, and continued my zigzagging mission.

Several family names triggered memories: Gartside, Entwistle, Harrington, Dixon.

Harper. Major Harper. Survived a war and died of flu!

Pritchard! Mr Pritchard. There he was:

> Robert Owen Pritchard
> 1900–1978
> Headmaster of Eldon Primary School
> 1940–1964
> His wife Evelyn
> 1903–1974
> Their dearly beloved son Robert
> 1923–1944,
> died at Anzio, grave unknown,
> serving his country

Did he ever travel to Italy to find his son's grave, I wondered? Did mother and father go together? With no grave, where would they grieve? Did he find anywhere, anything, to anchor his memories to? All through my schooldays when he listed the kings and queens of England, the prime numbers, the names of geometrical shapes, the capital cities of Europe; when he described battles, recited poems, celebrated anniversaries; when he took us for nature rambles and refereed the football matches on the school field – all this time he was carrying a terrible hurt within him. I didn't know any of this. Would I have been better behaved in his lessons if I had known? I like to think so, but I doubt it.

It was time to move on, but another name struck home. Patrick Wilfrid Dobson. And beneath his name, two others. His loving wife Florence and their beloved son, Harold Wilfrid, killed in action, 1941.

Harold Wilfrid Dobson. Uncle Harry! Wilfrid. That's who he was. It was a family name passed from father to son. But Harry hadn't had any children, so Dad gave it to me to carry the name on. Wilfrid. Your name still lives. I'm carrying it. I could start to use it again. In my new role!

And Patrick Dobson. PD. The initials on the screwdriver. They weren't Auntie Pauline's; they were those of her father-in-law. That was a relief; perhaps their relationship was innocent after all.

Among the chippings was a vase, currently empty. Did Auntie Pauline come down here and put flowers in that vase, flowers from her own garden, flowers that Dad had grown? Or did Dad put them there after paying his weekly visit to Auntie Pauline's or the Legion across the road? Both had a reason for this ritual.

When I left home a generation previously, I was hoping to cut the strings that were keeping me here. I was fighting to be free. But here in this gallery of lost life, I was still tied to the village, but not now by lack of ambition, but by memory, to these many graves. Invisible threads anchored me to these gloomy memorials. It was a fleeting feeling brought on by the atmosphere that graveyards create: loss, sadness, despair, loneliness, fear, hopelessness. Memorials that were meant to be a celebration were often the reverse.

But I couldn't avoid the real reason for my visit. It was easy enough to find, being the only freshly dug grave in sight. There was no stone yet, only some temporary marker. Beyond his grave was another which had not been obvious at the ceremony. Perhaps it had been covered by the tarpaulin that had earlier protected Dad's plot from rain. Within its marble frame was a little posy of primrose plants, no flowers yet but its leaves gathering strength to protect the flowers against the winter weather. Perhaps a relative had put it there earlier today. I looked at the name on the headstone.

Percy Swindells. Of course! When I was young, I thought he had the best job in the world. I wanted to do it when I left school. He drove the council steamroller. It was a monster, a big roller at the front, a tall chimney from the boiler, hissing pistons, whirring belt drives. Whenever it passed along the road, people would stop to watch it like it was an ancient warrior going to war. Mr Swindells would sit in his cab giving the whistle a sharp burst, whether as a warning or just to announce his arrival was never clear. The ground shivered with its power. And Percy was now dead. A job vacancy. I don't think so.

You don't come across many boys called Percy now. Dad's generation had a clutch of names that marked them out – Eric, Victor, Ernest, Harold, Gilbert, Wilfrid – all gone to be replaced by others more in fashion. My thoughts came back to Dad.

I thought of removing one of the primrose plants and putting it on Dad's grave. But that wouldn't have been right, would it? Anyway, the soil covering Dad wouldn't be there much longer. I'd ask Mam to see to it.

Who was going to arrange for a headstone? Surely, he hadn't carved one for himself. He was a wood man, not stone. I expected Stevens & Son had the answer.

This was the last time I would be close to Dad, and I wanted to say something. I knew what I wanted to say, but I hadn't formed the words to say it. It didn't occur to me as I was growing up, but I could see now. You were reliable, straightforward, hard-working, honest. You praised my skills, and you tolerated my weaknesses. I admired you. I respected you. But what I actually said was much simpler.

I loved you. What does that mean, son to father? You and Mam were the perfect parents – supportive, loving, generous… yet you fucked Auntie Pauline, Dad! How could you do that?

But I knew.

I leant forwards and picked up a ball of soil that had rolled away from the grave and threw it back on top – on top of the soil, on top of the beautifully constructed coffin, on top of the white cloth, on top of Dad.

I'd come back home to say farewell to this man who had meant so much – my idol, my ideal. But I was going away with a big black mark against his name.

He'd betrayed Mam. He'd fucked Auntie Pauline. He'd ruined everything for me. What had I got left? Not even self-respect.

★★★

I stood at Sally's door.

'Can I come in?' I didn't think she'd say yes, but she held the door open.

'What would you like? I'm making a pot of tea for myself.'

'That'll do fine.' I lied so easily.

'How did it go yesterday?'

'As you'd expect really.' I didn't tell her about Mam and Auntie Pauline.

'Your mother taking it alright?'

I nodded. 'I'm sorry about walking off the other day. You caught me on the raw.'

'We all have off days.'

I had to ask her. What did she really know? What really happened? I didn't come straight out. She might know nothing. There might be nothing to know.

'What you were saying the other day. About that woman staying loyal to her dead boyfriend. Does it happen? Much?'

'More than you can imagine. You and your view of women. I try to be faithful, but as you know, I don't always succeed.' She caught my eye and laughed. A real easy-going noise. But it was like a match to petrol. I wanted her. Oh yes, I wanted her. 'Now, now.' She sensed my move before I made it and stood up to get the tea.

When she returned, I said, 'Seriously. You think it could happen. Complete faithfulness, I mean. Well, it does happen a lot if you're to be believed.'

'Why shouldn't it? Love, honour and obey. It's the decent thing, isn't it. If you're not loyal, why should anybody be loyal to you?'

'But you're talking about women. Can men be loyal?'

She turned away and said, 'It would be nice to think they could be.'

'But are they? Your old man doesn't have much choice unless…'

She turned back and her eyes were moist. 'No. I don't think some men can be. Look at you.'

'I didn't mean me. Let me put it this way. Supposing a man regularly saw a woman. Someone who wasn't his wife. In her own home, say. For year after year. Surely, they must be having sex.'

'Probably.'

'But not necessarily?'

'No. What sort of man have you in mind?'

'Well, no one really. It's sort of hypothetical, if you like.'

'Is this hypothetical man happily married?'

I really had to think about that after all that had happened. 'Yes.'

'And the woman?'

Christ, what was I to say? If I said no, she'd want to know more. It would all come out. 'The husband's out of the frame. Like yours.'

'You're not talking about you and me, are you?'

'No, no. Just using your situation.'

'What's the woman like?'

'How do you mean?'

'Well, is she nice? Is she sexy? Is she selfish?'

'Yes. No. No.'

'You know this hypothetical woman very well, don't you.'

'No. No.'

'Peter. You're as transparent as an empty pint glass.'

'How do you mean?'

'You want to know if your dad was shagging Mrs Dobson, don't you?'

I was glad she said that. I needed a direct answer. Nobody would give it to me. She would. It was my turn to look away. 'It would help.'

'I don't know,' she replied, after a pause.

Well, that wasn't very useful!

'Do you think he *could* have been?'

'Yes, but it doesn't mean he was.'

'What do the gossips say? In the pub? Howard?'

'Howard has never said anything. He's not that kind of man.'

'Would Howard have done something like that?'

'You mean if Howard was married and just happened to visit a woman friend every week to help with her gardening, would he have slept with her? This is going to require some imagination, isn't it? This is ridiculous. You see your dad and Howard the same because they're both men. You don't see them as two different people. You think they're going to think and behave just like you.'

'Well to some extent yes. We've got the same urges?'

'You think so.'

'Well, I'm not sure about Howard. He keeps himself to himself. Lives with his mother. No girlfriends. I suppose he's queer.'

'You're pathetic. Howard's not queer.'

'How do you know?'

'Women can tell these things.' Women!

'I suppose you've slept with him. On one of your needy days, I expect.'

'That's really out of order. Look, I'm getting pissed off with you. You came here wanting sympathy. Fair enough. I feel sorry for you. Genuinely sorry. But you wouldn't know about that. I think you should go.'

But she hadn't told me. I still needed to know. I got up to leave. As I turned to face her, I found myself looking through the kitchen window beyond her garden and straight at the leylandii fringing Auntie Pauline's garden, hiding everything from view. I left with nothing else said.

★★★

Supper was a subdued affair. I couldn't get Sally out of my mind. Not so much Sally herself, more the comments she had made about me. I suppose I was ignoring Mam. My mind came back to her when I noticed a framed photo of Dad on the mantelpiece. It hadn't been there before, had it? I turned my chair to look around the room to see if there were any more, me perhaps. There was a black-and-white photo of the three of us at some seaside promenade. Mam saw me looking at it.

'Do you remember where that was?'

I looked to be about nine years old and had a guess. 'New Brighton?'

'Blackpool.' Then I saw the tower in the background.

'Oh, yes. Who took that then?'

'Just some man doing it for a living.'

I didn't remember the incident. I did remember slides and merry-go-rounds, stalls selling little cartons of shrimps, kiosks with whiskery candyfloss. I recalled too, strong waves beating against the promenade walls, drenching the visitors who had gathered there deliberately to get wet, it seemed. But was that Blackpool, or Whitby, or Rhyl, or any of the dozen resorts we had been to? We never missed a summer. I switched my gaze back to Dad. Mam was looking at him too.

'Why have you put that up now?'

'I didn't need to before. He was always here. Now I need to be reminded of what he looked like. I've got some more photos of him if you'd like. I know you were very close.'

'Yes, we had some great times.'

'You didn't spend much time with *me*, did you? Just the two of us I mean.'

She was right of course. I could see that, looking back. How clear things are when you look back.

'I had a life, you know, even after you were born, but before that as well. You don't know any of it, and when I die, you won't have my life to keep alive.'

I asked did she want to tell me about it, but I hadn't reckoned how much detail there would be. She had been born in a little village about eight miles away. It was on a minor road towards the hills; I had never been there. At fourteen she went to work at Eldon Manor as a maid; later the house became The Manor Hotel on the Wellworth Road, but back then it was owned by the Borthwick family. It was there she met Auntie Pauline who did the same work. They lived in. Once a week, the two of them would go to the dance at the parish hall which was knocked down later when the community hall was built after the war. Here they met Dad – Eric – and Harry Dobson. They soon paired off and, before long, the two men would escort their girlfriends back to The Manor. There was no intimacy; both girls would lose their jobs if Lady Borthwick found out. Eric and Harry were local boys, and any misbehaviour would soon get back to their parents.

'Why did you choose Dad instead of Harry?'

'Pauline and I didn't have a competition. We each seemed drawn to different boys. I seemed more at ease with Eric. He lived with his parents in one of those cottages that we lived in after you were born; the ones that were knocked down when we moved here. His dad was a dairyman at Burton's Farm. There was a simplicity about Eric that seem to suggest I would be safe with him.'

Safe?

'So, Auntie Pauline and Harry became an item?'

'Yes. They were well suited too. Harry lived with his parents in the house where Pauline lives now. His father was the secretary of Fincham Golf Club. He wasn't an easy man to like. But Harry, like the rest of us, didn't have a choice over his parents. Harry was a class above Eric, and Pauline liked that.'

'So, Auntie Pauline and you got what you wanted.'

'The four of us were great friends; there was no jealousy, no disagreements.'

Dad had started work at Bennett's the joiners, and Harry worked as a clerk in the office of a local solicitor. They seemed to have life sorted when the war came along. If they had paid more attention to the news, it might have been anticipated, but they were only twenty-year-olds, and Europe seemed another world.

It came as a shock to Mam and Auntie Pauline when Eric and Harry reported they had been called up to join the army. The two couples had been on one of their walks on Leaden Hill. There were boulders on the top, and they sat looking over the surrounding countryside. It was Harry who broke the news, and he seemed to have more enthusiasm. Eric would have gone along with it, as he and Harry were best mates.

'Harry was acting a little strangely. He looked out over the countryside and said that he didn't want to die here; he needed to get away.'

I knew what he meant. Mam couldn't understand that. The four of them had a nice existence and prospects – homes and families. Why give that up? And what's the point of getting away if you're going to get killed? The two couples came down the mountain arm in arm, except where the track narrowed and the men held out their hands to guide their partners over the uneven surface. Mam said Dad didn't say much, but it seemed to her he was holding her hand more tightly than usual.

It then happened quickly. The men joined up with the same regiment. They had leave for Christmas and then Easter. At Easter Mam and Dad got married and went to live with Dad's mother in the two-up-two down cottage on Leaden Hill Road. In the summer, Harry and Auntie Pauline got married and went to live with his parents. Then Harry was killed.

'By then I was pregnant,' said Mam. I had to get into this story sometime. 'But I didn't tell Eric straight away. When Harry died, I was forever anxious that the same might happen to Eric. Once you were born, and later Eric came back from the war, we settled, here in Eldon, and lived quietly.'

'But there was a lot left of your life, and we did live a quiet life for a long time.'

'We can talk about that tomorrow.'

'I'm supposed to be seeing Auntie Pauline tomorrow.'

'We can go together. She can pick up the story.'

The story! So, there was more then… what?

SUNDAY

Most days in my life have been predictable – apart from the orders, obviously. I leave the house, get in my car and off I go, to different places admittedly, but the same routine. If I'm not staying away for the night, I'm home by seven and Maureen will have a nice meal waiting. The kids will have eaten earlier; Mam, Dad and me always ate our meals together, but it's a different world now. Maureen handles all the household stuff, insurance, rates and so on. And she does all the shopping, even since she's started work. So, my life is pretty easy. I do the garden though, claiming I have the skill to look after it properly. I have Dad to thank there. There must be the odd day when I don't know how the day will map out – three job interviews and two court appearances over the years – but it's usually plain sailing. And it has been like that for twenty years.

This day it was to be different. To say I sensed it as soon as I woke up would be to dramatise it overmuch, and to claim insight when looking back would give me psychic powers I don't have. But inside, something nagged away. It must have been Mam's remark about Auntie Pauline picking up the story. What story? Whose story?

The plan for the morning was easy enough: up to Auntie Pauline's with Mam for a chat. Perhaps she would reveal some part of her life I knew nothing about. She wasn't going to confess about her and Dad, surely? What would be the point? My mind kept making up little stories that might fit the facts as I knew them, but I abandoned them as soon as they became absurd.

At about nine-thirty, we set off for Auntie Pauline's. There was an autumn chill about, but it wasn't raining. When you live in a small community and don't have a car to hold your attention, you inevitably pass places that arouse some sort of memory, and so it was this day – the bus stop where we waited for the school bus each morning copying homework and taunting the girls, the postbox where I posted orders for a special cream that would eliminate blackheads, the old filling station abandoned to the receiver now, the road to The Anchor where furtive sallies turned in time into blatant intentions, the road to Sally's which I tried not to look down, the school where we burned up the energy in our bodies with little to show in our minds. And then we were there: Auntie Pauline's. What now?

The door to the garage at the side of the house was open, and I could see a car. I could see from the number plate it was quite old, unless she had moved the registration plate from one new model to another, but there was nothing distinctive about the characters to make that worthwhile.

Auntie Pauline let us in and took us through to her back room, overlooking the garden. Was this deliberate?

Mam and Auntie Pauline seemed at ease with each other, almost as if they knew what was to come. I didn't know, and I felt awkward. Auntie Pauline went out to make some tea. While she was doing so, I looked around the room. There were more photos than I had noticed before, many of me with Mam and Dad, Dad and Harry in uniform. Two of couples in a pair of wedding photographs with best men and bridesmaids; it had to be Mam and Dad, Harry and Auntie Pauline, but the quality of the prints made them difficult to recognise. As soon as I recognised Dad, the others fell into place. Auntie Pauline was a good-looking woman, nearly as tall as Harry. I supposed Harry might have been on the small side.

After Auntie Pauline had handed out the teacups, there was silence, as though each was waiting for the other.

Mam broke the ice and said, 'I've been telling Peter about our lives before the war. I stopped at the point when Harry was killed as I thought you would like to pick it up there.' It sounded like a sentence that had been rehearsed.

Auntie Pauline took up the story, 'Well, we'd only just got married. We should have been happy, and we were for only a few days. It was a Saturday afternoon if you remember. Eric and Harry had gone back to their camp early that morning. Quite by chance, we had gone to church, something was on, it wasn't a service, I don't remember now. The vicar came over to us. He looked very shaken. He was one of the few people in the village who had a phone, and Eric had called him. He told me Harry had been killed, but he didn't know any more. He said Eric was coming straight back, but maybe couldn't make it until the next day. I was confused. It was wartime. Harry was in the army, but he was still in this country. How could he be killed? What would happen to me?'

Sensing Auntie Pauline's distress, Mam took up the story. The next day, Eric arrived, and he and Mam went up to Auntie Pauline's. Eric described how, before he and Harry reported back to barracks, they went for a drink. Neither of them was used to heavy drinking. Whether it was that, or perhaps the beer they were drinking was stronger than usual, but when they got outside, they were both unsteady. Harry slung his knapsack over his back and the momentum took him into the road. He was hit by a passing milk truck and knocked down. He wasn't dead, and Eric stayed with him, waiting for an ambulance to arrive. Eric kept talking, trying to keep Harry conscious, and it was then that Harry asked Eric to look after Auntie Pauline if he didn't make it. As the ambulance crew were just about to pick up the stretcher with Harry on it, he breathed his last, and as Eric was often heard to say, "He died just there," not on the field of battle but in the gutter of a small English town. It wasn't very glorious.

I recalled the writing on Harry's grave: *Killed in action*. Hardly that, but I suppose people can inscribe what they like on a gravestone. Harry's parents knew what they wanted it to say and instructed the mason to add that to their names when they went. It was some years before

Harry's mother died, so it wasn't until the fifties that the slogan actually appeared. His name was on the war memorial between the church and The Church Inn, and that was enough. I wondered how many people in the village knew the truth, or did they honour this fallen soldier with as much reverence as those who had died on the beaches on D-Day or at Dunkirk, or fell from the sky in a blazing bomber. The people in the village knew what they wanted to believe, and it was best left at that. Just like they knew what they wanted to believe about Dad and Auntie Pauline!

Harry's father could not cope with his loss. He had served throughout the Great War and, in one campaign, had survived for twelve hours in a foxhole. These experiences had left their mark; depression distorted his mind and intensified as he got older. A few days after Harry's death, he was found one morning, dead in one of the bunkers at the golf course, killed by a single bullet from his service revolver. Was his death in this suburban foxhole symbolic or accidental? Did he fall into the sandy pit, or did he place himself there, submitting to the death he had escaped a generation before? Did he leave this world behind dismayed that his country was embarking on a second war when the lessons of the first were so stark, or ashamed of the tawdriness of his son's death? Only he knew, and the coroner drew no conclusions for motive. Auntie Pauline was left living with Harry's mother, and the two of them existed in a state of emotional tension for the next ten years.

I was beginning to relax as the conversation seemed little more than interesting family history. It was soon to take a more dramatic line. Auntie Pauline took up the story.

'I knew I was pregnant by several months on my wedding day. The baby must have been conceived when Eric and Harry came home for Eric's wedding to you, Margery. What was I to do now? I was a widow with no income, a soon-to-be mother with no husband, and I was living with my in-laws. Mrs Dobson would soon work out the baby had been conceived months before we were married, and she had a very traditional view of marriage. Mr Dobson's suicide was the final straw. Margery and I had a long chat over many days, didn't we, Margery?'

'Yes, it was a bit hectic, but we were strong-minded, so we had to get on with it. Unfortunately, we had more to cope with. I had been pregnant and had written to tell Eric. What I didn't tell him about was the miscarriage, which was just after Harry died and Eric had returned to camp,' intervened Mam.

A miscarriage. That was me, wasn't it?

'But what to do about Auntie Pauline's baby? We thought it best that nobody in Eldon knew about it. We decided to get well away until the baby was born. We had a friend who ran a B&B in Morecambe – she used to be a cook at The Manor – and it would be cheap enough to stay there out of season. We both had a little saved up.'

'But it took us a little time to work out what to do about the baby. Could it be adopted? We didn't really contemplate abortion then. In the end, Margery offered to look after it, pretending it was her own. After all she had been pregnant, so the deceit might have gone unnoticed.'

I didn't like where this was going.

'After the birth, we went to the register office and registered the birth in my name, with Pauline as a witness.'

'I had a nasty feeling the registrar would not believe us, even though this sort of thing must have been going on all the time.'

'In Morecambe?'

'Even in Morecambe.'

'Nobody was going to check up; there was a war on.'

'Well, the registrar let it go through, whether through trust or charity I couldn't say.'

'So, in January 1942, you were registered as Peter Wilfrid Carter, son of Eric and Margery. Wilfrid, after Harry's father, your grandfather. It was quite common then for boys to be named after their granddads.'

They were both looking at me, expecting a response, I supposed, but my mind wouldn't work. I got out of my chair. My mind was reeling. I couldn't face this. I went out of the back door and lit up a fag. I sat on the back steps, looking out over the garden. My head was all over the place. This was the garden that Dad had maintained for over forty years. Except he wasn't my father. Harry was, if I'd followed the story. And Auntie Pauline was my mother. *Is* my mother! Not "Mam" of course but my mother nevertheless. Mam and Dad had brought me up as their own son and given me all those years of love and security; had that now gone? Who were Mam and Dad now? I went back inside.

I looked at both women. Who was my mother? What did that mean? I didn't know anymore. They were sitting either side of me and simultaneously put their hands over each of mine. Were they both claiming me? Did I have to choose between them?

Harry wasn't a war hero, but was Dad? I'd seen him in uniform. I'd seen his medals. I'd examined his tattoo. I'd heard his stories... Dad was a war hero, or was he? Was there another twist to this story? Did I want to know what they'd told me, or did I wish I was still ignorant of it all? I had no choice. It had been revealed. It couldn't be unsaid, undone. Was I a different person because of this?

'This is all a bit confusing. Why did you tell me? Wouldn't it have been better to keep it hidden?'

'We didn't want to do it while Eric was still alive. He believed you were his son. It would have been unnecessarily upsetting to tell him,' Mam explained.

So, for all those years, Mam was lying to Dad, or at least not telling the truth. This big thing lay between them – known to Mam, hidden from Dad. Yet they seemed so comfortable, so right, together. How did Mam cope with that? Mam?

Auntie Pauline – my mother now – chipped in with, 'And if we'd told you, it would have got back to him, as these things do.'

The strongest link between me and Dad – the bloodline – was an illusion. But those connections we did have – the woodwork lessons in the garage, the cigarettes at the bottom of the garden, the trips up Leaden Hill, the sandcastles on the beach – they were all real because we both believed them to be true. They *were* real. They couldn't be taken away, whatever the record showed. There was only one real father: Dad.

'We told you because you have many years to live. You might find out at any time. We might not have been around to tell you the true story. It's better out now.'

'And you can see we, both your mothers, love you as our own.'

They both squeezed my hands, simultaneously it seemed.

'But you had a fight, or at least a disagreement.'

Auntie Pauline said, 'It was nothing really, but let me explain. For the first two years after you were born, we both looked after you in a way. Don't forget Eric was away in the war. I would come down to your house, and we would wheel you in your pram up to the church and back – further if the weather was good. We were like a young married couple. I would often feed you and change your nappies. I would sing you songs and rhymes that I had been taught as a child. We didn't come to this house because Mrs Dobson was a nosey old so-and-so. But then you started to speak and began to call Margery "Mam". I found that very hard. We decided I would keep out of your life for your sake. Then Eric was demobbed, and there was no going back.'

'Did Dad know any of this?' I couldn't stop calling him "Dad". I wasn't going to.

The two women looked at each other. Auntie Pauline replied. I wasn't going to stop calling her "Auntie Pauline" and I certainly wasn't going to be calling her "Mother". And as for Mam, there was only one Mam. Wasn't there?

'We decided it would do more harm than good. It was our secret – until now.'

'Dad died believing you were his son, and he took all those memories of things you shared with him. They were real memories, weren't they? Real to him and real to you, if you keep it that way. He can still be your hero.'

'And I was your son too?'

'Of course,' said Mam.

'You could have two mothers, if you wanted,' said Auntie Pauline, looking directly at me.

I was looking straight into her eyes, and they were my eyes – the ones that stared back from the shaving mirror. For the first time, I began to wonder what she made of it all.

'I used to send Pauline photos we took of you – some on holiday and some taken by the school. I used to walk up to Pauline's when I took you to school and push them through her letterbox. Later, when Dad began to look after the garden, he took them up. I don't think he had any suspicions.'

'I used to keep them in albums. They're in that bureau over there,' Pauline said, pointing behind me. 'When you went to school, I used to keep watch at the beginning and the end of the day as well as break times, hoping I would catch a glimpse of you to add to my photographic memories.'

The twitching curtains then.

So, for a decade, she had lived apart from me, unable to comfort me, to encourage me, to applaud me, to scold me; yet she had held me inside her for nine months, given birth to me. But for half of that time, I had come up with Dad every Sunday morning when we did her garden. I had been physically so close to her, yet mostly ignored her, making only those superficial contacts that usually occur between a youngster and an adult. Was she making a sacrifice, her sacrifice, for me, like Mam had sacrificed her freedom in our family home? Which was the greater, I wondered? Better to see them as equal.

'When Harry's mother died – you would have just begun secondary school – I wanted to tell you the whole story. After all, I had spent ten years without you, unable to kiss your cheek, to give you a hug. I would spend the rest of my life alone. That would have been so hard. It *has* been so hard. But it was for you. Mothers make all kinds of different sacrifices for their children. Margery and I each made our own. It must have been then you stopped coming with Eric. With Mrs Dobson gone and you no longer in the school across the road, I was really on my own. I asked Margery to tell you then, but looking back I can see that wasn't sensible. We fell out. I guess we both said things we regretted soon after, regret now certainly. Fortunately, Eric continued to come. It was a big comfort.'

'How did you cope?'

'I pulled myself together. Isn't that what women are supposed to do? I bought a car and learnt to drive. After I passed my test, I had a freedom I hadn't had before. I used to take little trips out, find a little café or sit somewhere with a good view. I would read a lot. I often thought of bringing your photo albums to leaf through, but I was trying to escape you, wasn't I? Escape your absence would be more accurate. That little car was a lifeline. It's in the garage out there now. I still use it. I could have got a job, but I didn't need the money. I think that was a mistake. It meant I turned in on myself, allowing self-pity to get a hold. I shrivelled when I could have blossomed. It stunted my own life and for no good reason, but I had no one to help me out of it. In time, Margery came to my rescue.'

It was Mam's turn. 'After you left home, and before Dad became too ill for me to leave him, Pauline and I used to meet up for a chat. You know that lane that runs down over there?' She was pointing beyond the leylandii to the lane that ran past Sally's. 'Well, it leads into the fields behind The Manor where we first met. There used to be a tree trunk that had fallen down and made a nice little seat. Not many people came that way; the lane doesn't lead anywhere, so we had our private spot. We took it in turns to bring something to drink and a little snack. Every Monday morning after Dad had gone to work, I would phone Pauline and we would decide what to do and which day to do it. Eric knew nothing of this. It was something the two of us had between us.'

'Did you talk about me?' I asked, hopefully.

'Well of course, but you weren't the only thing in our lives. Just across the field was Eldon Manor where we spent a lot of time together when we were in service before we got married. And there were plenty of stories to tell. There was a man there who was the butler, Robinson I think.'

'No, Robertson,' intervened Pauline.

'Yes. Robertson. He had a glass eye; lost it in the war we think. But he never missed a trick. Could spot a dusty surface a mile off.'

'And you had to be careful not to be in a room on

your own with him. His hands wandered as much as his good eye.'

'So, you see we had plenty to talk about.'

'But I was always back home when Eric came home for dinner.'

'Later, when I got my car, and I became a more confident driver, we used to go out for the whole day and have lunch at some country café far away.'

'On those days, I used to tell Eric I was going off to the shops in Cooksley, which was partly true. I always left him something to eat though.'

'I don't think he ever suspected.'

'He didn't say anything to me.'

A clock chimed midday somewhere in Auntie Pauline's house.

'Come on, it's time to go. Howard's picking you up later, isn't he?'

As we were standing on her step turning to go, Auntie Pauline said, 'Can I ask you, Peter? Will you remember me? Not as your mother perhaps, but not a stranger. When you send your Christmas cards and holiday postcards, don't forget me. You don't owe me anything, but I gave a lot up for you. I'm not being a martyr, but I don't want to be forgotten. So, remember me.'

I knew what she meant. I went down the two steps to the path and turned to look back at her. I looked at her face. It was my face, wasn't it? I went back up the steps, and as I held her in my arms, I could feel her choking back tears. If I hadn't done it then, I might never have done it. Perhaps I'd changed. In those two weeks I had changed. In those two hours I had changed even more.

We did not speak as we walked home. Mam held my hand, and I didn't object. I could understand the history of what I'd just been told but was having a lot of difficulty with the shift in relationships that were a consequence. This woman, holding my hand, like she did when she was Mam, was *not* my mother. That woman who we had just left, who had been a figure of suspicion and distrust, *was* my mother. How could I adjust to all that? Did I need to rethink every encounter I had had with them, clear every emotion? That would be impossible; they were fixed in me. They were what gave my childhood stability; they still did.

And that man who was Dad, who gave me so much of his time, was *not* my father. What *was* he then? He was at least a war hero, wasn't he? They can't take that away. Then my birth father – not Dad – lying in the grave for over forty years, had been killed by a milk wagon. He had seen no war action, had not even been overseas. He had not given me anything. How should I think of *him*? I couldn't feel anything; he was just a rotting body in Eldon churchyard. He died before I was born; he gave me nothing – no image, no memory, no feeling. Auntie Pauline… not "Mam" surely… had pictures of him. I had seen them, blurred black-and-white images. What a flimsy connection. At least he knew nothing of this, didn't even know he was a father. Poor Harry. Poor… who?

My thoughts evaporated when we arrived home. No, not evaporated, congealed inside me. We had my favourite lunch of egg, sausage, beans, tea and buttered bread. She remembered. Of course she did.

I had to ask her, 'What did Uncle Harry look like?' I couldn't think of him as my father. He would still be Uncle Harry, and Dad would be "Dad".

She moved to the cupboards neatly built into the alcove alongside the chimney breast. Dad had built them, of course. She took out a shoebox and put it on the table in front of me.

'All the pictures in there were taken before you were born. Harry will be in there together with Pauline, Dad and me. It's our lives when we were young and free and optimistic. You will see Harry as he might have been for you.'

'Can I take these with me?'

'No, you would be taking my life. You can pick one of Harry, perhaps Harry and Pauline together, and take that. You can have the rest when I've gone.'

The one I chose had them arm in arm, sitting on a sea wall. Those two had created me. Could I see myself in them? I believed I could, but sentiment allows you to believe anything you like. Was that really Auntie Pauline? It was Auntie Pauline, before forty years of sadness had taken its toll.

And this was Harry. Nothing to compare him with. What could I see in him? He looked happy, but if you can't look happy in a holiday photograph, you've got problems.

Slightly full-faced. That fitted me.

Lots of hair. Can't have everything.

I propped the photo against my teacup, its bottom edge resting on the saucer.

'I'd like this, thanks… I don't know what to call

them. You and Dad were "Mam" and "Dad"; I'd like to keep that. But I have to use different words for them. What do you think?'

'I don't know, but one day it will come to you. Until then, Uncle Harry and Auntie Pauline will do. Only the three of us know anything different.'

Maureen has a friend who lets her children call her and her husband by their Christian names. I couldn't possibly call mine Eric and Margery. She put the box back in the cupboard, and I noticed how smoothly the doors closed. Well done, Dad.

I remembered the gravestone and asked Mam if she had any plans. She said Dad had put a bit of money away. I didn't think I could bring up the matter of primroses. There was time for that.

'What are you going to do now, Mam?'

'I'll cope same as I've always done. First, I'm going to do up the front bedroom, get rid of that old bed, have the room redecorated.'

'I'll give Gary a call. He's a painter and decorator, but make sure they respect Dad's handiwork. Don't let them spread paint over everything.'

'I might get a little part-time job. They're looking for check-out staff at the little supermarket.'

'There's no need for that. I can help you out with a little money.' Assuming I still had a job that was.

'It's not the money. I don't have any rent to pay ever since we bought this house.'

'Bought it?'

'Yes. Some years ago, five or six, the government let council tenants buy their own houses. We only had to pay part of its value. Dad had some money saved up, and we borrowed a bit. All paid off now. So, after thirty years of paying someone to live in *their* house, we had a house of our own. You couldn't imagine how wonderful that was.'

'But you never told me.'

'Well, Dad was a bit secretive about money matters. You'll learn more when you read the will.'

Here was something else she had held back. What else might there be? So, I'll come into some money when Mam's gone. I might be glad of it then. He wouldn't have left it to someone else surely – Auntie Pauline, the British Legion?

'So, you can live comfortably here?'

'Yes, we were joint owners, and I will inherit his share. So, it will all come into my name. You can't imagine what it feels like to be secure. When Pauline and I started working in Eldon Manor before the war, we would often talk about our dreams of owning our own home, a nice husband, two or three children. It hasn't quite worked out like that, but they were dreams, weren't they? The reality turned out a little different.'

'So, you're secure here for the rest...'

'Yes, but I don't want to be tied to this place. Not forever. Remember, when you and Dad were doing all those things together, I was stuck in here making sure things were just right when you came home. I didn't resent it, because I saw it as my duty. Duty as wife and mother. And duty to Pauline too – you were her child, and I held you in trust. You came to respect Dad for all the things he did with you, and you seemed to ignore all the things I did. Your favourite meals, your clothes washed and ironed, your forehead mopped when you had a fever once, the visits to school to see your teachers when you misbehaved.'

She was right, of course. I could see that. But I couldn't change it. I could change me perhaps, but from what to what? I couldn't face these uncomfortable truths. I dodged them as usual.

Just as I thought it was safe to leave, Mam came up with something else.

'Pauline and I think we might live together. For company. We don't need two houses. If we only had one, we'd have a bit of money and could enjoy ourselves. Have some nice holidays.' Morecambe perhaps!

'Which house would you choose?'

'We haven't decided yet. Hers is bigger than this one, and it would be nice to have more space.'

'But if you moved from here, I'd have no home to come back to.'

'Don't be daft. You'd be coming home to me – to us. I'd only be moving a quarter of a mile. You'd still have a home.'

It all made sense of course, but we're generally not keen on people upsetting our lives even when it improves theirs. But wouldn't Sally be next door? She might have gone back to her husband, but perhaps not.

'I'll just go and finish packing. Howard will be here soon.'

I stood up to go and she did at the same time. Suddenly we were close, not just physically close, but close in some other way too. I put my arms around her shoulders, pulling her towards me. I said, 'You'll always... be... Mam... to me.' I couldn't complete the sentence without sobbing, and the shoulder of her dress – her best Sunday dress – became soaked in my tears. I pulled away without looking into her face. What stopped me?

Upstairs, I put the photo in a side pocket of my raincoat. I had previously packed my stuff – a few clothes, Uncle Harry's screwdriver, Dad's medals. I looked around the room, but there was nothing more I wanted to take. Through the window, I could see Howard's Rover pull up. Going in style, eh. I went downstairs.

'Thanks, Mam... for everything.'

I should have said more. I wanted to say more. Was it true of all families that however much they cared for each other, however much they shared the little things, they couldn't talk about the big things? Or was that just me and my family? And I couldn't share this with Maureen and the kids. It had to remain a secret between me and... another family secret, not to be shared.

I had just put my bag in Howard's car when I thought of one last thing. 'Hang on a minute, Howard.'

I walked down the side of the house where we used to repair bikes, passed the garage where I learnt to saw, down the garden to the little bench at the bottom where we used to chat and secretly smoke our cigarettes. I stood in front of the bench, hidden from the house by bushes now thinning at the onset of winter.

'Thanks, Dad... for everything.'

As I stood looking at the bench, I could see the

varnish was peeling off one of the seat slats and the wood beneath was beginning to rot. Are memories going to fade just like the varnish on the seat, leaving the lived life to rot away? I sighed – at what, the past or the future?

I returned to join Howard, waiting patiently at the front of the house. As the car pulled away, I could see Mam in the side mirror, standing on the front step, and an idea struck me.

'Howard. Will you do me a favour? Will you just run us round the village past all the places we used to play? Just for old times' sake.'

Howard looked at me, then smiled and nodded.

As we came back from the church end of the village, our house was on my side of the car. Mam had gone inside, but as we approached, I saw her at the front bedroom window pulling the curtains apart and opening the windows wide. She waved as we passed. Spring cleaning, eh, Mam. Well, autumn cleaning. But what are you cleaning out? Not me, I hope. Not me.

Howard turned up the Wellworth Road and then right towards Leaden Hill. We passed the end of Sally's road. It was Sunday lunchtime. Would she be on duty at The Manor? No matter.

'Did you take your mother for Sunday lunch at The Manor, Howard? You usually do.'

'Yes. I did my duty.'

Duty. It was better than that, Howard.

'Was Sally there?'

'Yes, she was behind the front desk.' I didn't dare ask if she'd said anything.

Auntie Pauline's house was next, and I remembered some of the conversation that morning. She *had* said something, and no mistake.

On the right was the school, dormant on this Sunday afternoon but alive with memories.

'I don't think we'll go any further. Not to Manor Meadows or the railway line,' decided Howard.

'No, you're right. We have to be choosy with our memories.'

★★★

I bought a pint for myself and a tonic for Howard. We were in The George and had just made the three o'clock deadline. Howard must have put his foot down, but in his Rover it didn't seem fast. But Howard wouldn't speed, would he?

'You've had quite an eventful fortnight, Peter. Is it what you expected?'

'No. It's been quite upsetting in many ways, not just Dad.' I had to be careful not to let anything slip about Auntie Pauline.

'Meeting with Gary and Bendy didn't go too well, did it?' observed Howard. That was an understatement.

'Bendy upset me, I can't deny that. I was thinking the other night: why was it we called him Bendy? His real name was Benedict, wasn't it? Still, we were all mates.'

'Are we mates now?' asked Howard.

'Well, Gordon and Billy have gone. I'm not sure I want to be mates with Bendy.'

'So that leaves Gary and me. And Gary's tied up with

his four kids. So that just leaves you and me. Are we still mates then?' asked Howard, seeming to demand an answer.

Although I was slow to answer, I was sure of what I said.

'Yes. Yes. Of course. You've done a lot for me, especially these last two weeks. You've been a real mate. You've always been there.'

'But I'm always here, aren't I? Never moved,' he said ruefully.

'You said you were happy here.'

'Perhaps I meant not unhappy.'

'That might be good enough. Although I was desperate to get away from here, I'm not sure I was any happier for it.'

'Why?'

'Howard. Howard. Howard. I've always lived on the surface. Don't ask me to delve deep down inside myself. God knows what I'd find.'

'I've heard religious people say that's exactly what we have to do.'

I looked at the clock behind the bar and was relieved it was time to go. The George was close to the station so we could walk. We parted at the steps to the station. We shook hands. With some people I would have given them a hug, but Howard wasn't a hugging person, I assumed. Nor was I.

'I'll try to visit Mam a bit more often. When I do, I'll give you a ring and we can meet up.'

'Just us two?'

'We're all that's left.'

I went up the stairs to the platform as I had many times in the past, times when life was simple. Not now.

★★★

After an initial jolt, the train pulled smoothly out of the station that had been my gateway to and from childhood. I found a seat in a smoking compartment but took time to get out my cigarettes, the necessity dulled, the habit weakened. Now on my own for a while, I had time to think, to assemble the detail I had learnt that morning into focus. I'd had difficulty separating memory from reality, lies from truth.

I had to believe that Dad had never lied to me, because he didn't know there was anything about me to lie about, although some of his war stories may not have been the full truth. His one big war story must have been true as it was too important to invent. It had gone with him now, but he had left it to me, in part the facts of his own memory, but also the memory I have of him telling me the story. Looking back, I wondered if, in telling me, he recognised I was slipping away from him. No longer the youngster, but the growing adolescent with his own concerns.

However, he could have been hiding the truth about him and Auntie Pauline. I still don't know the truth of that. It could be true, but nothing I had heard that morning suggested it was, and I chose to deny it. So, all the memories I have of Dad remain unsullied, as close to reality as could be.

Mam had never lied to me, just not told the truth;

she did that to protect me. For over forty years, she had held back on what was a most personal and precious fact; she did not give birth to me. That must surely be love, love which expects no return but is rewarded when it is. What did I give her? Not much over my life, and just recently, I had blatantly lied to her, about Sally Ryan for instance. No pretence at just not telling the truth, an out-and-out lie to her face. And I had lied to protect myself. She'd lost a child, a child she didn't have chance to love. Instead, she gave that love to me. No, not "instead". She could love us both. It didn't take much insight to see how stressful that must have been. All the time she was caring for me, she must have been reminded of the child who wasn't there, Dad's child. If she did, I never felt denied her love, although she was a bit aloof at times. Not surprising really.

She was a Christian, of course, a churchgoer at least. But she didn't leave those beliefs at the church door. Her whole life seemed to give life to the lessons from the Bible, the teaching of the Church. And she gave love to me as well as her lost baby; was that another kind of love? Was it a boy, or a girl?

Maureen and I had lost a child between William and Claire. It was a boy. We didn't get time to name him; I don't think I'd have chosen Wilfrid, or even Eric. Sorry, Dad.

But Auntie Pauline had lost a child too. Her child had not been spirited out of sight in some graveyard or crematorium. He... I had been living a few hundred yards from her home. Every sight of me, in the school playground, shouting as I passed her front door with my mates as we went to Burton's field and the railway line, must have plucked some nerve, pressed on some bruise to remind her what she was missing. She hadn't lied to me as we had rarely spoken, but she had held in check a huge truth in order to protect me. I began to see the enormity of that. None of this was memory, but my attempt to understand her life. She deserved a place in my memory now. They'd made room for each other now, Auntie Pauline and Mam, both mothers to me. I should make room for both of them. But I didn't have memories of Auntie Pauline, other than the few I heard about this morning, but I could concoct others. It would seem strange, creating the life of a parent, something to fill a gap in my memory, but with no truth to it. They would be unreliable memories but might just seem real after regular recall.

Then I thought of the wider family. Maureen would be OK, but she probably knew the truth anyway; she hinted she did. But all of it? Dare I discuss this with her, or say nothing, not the truth but not lies? I decided to tell her all I knew. Not to do so would involve deception, and Maureen deserves better than that. I had memories of her I wanted to remember and memories of me I wanted to forget. I was coming home, Maureen.

William and Claire had got used to their grandparents being Mam and Dad. Other than seeing Auntie Pauline at the funeral, they'd never met her before. And their birth grandfather has lain in the graveyard since before they were born. To land them with this confusion would be unnecessarily disturbing at the very time of their lives when they crave certainty. So, for *them* no truth then, but no lies either. I thought I might write out my life story and attach it to my will, so they would know the truth eventually. By then, all Mam and Dad's generation would be long gone and most of mine as well. As mature adults, William and Claire would be able to deal with this, wouldn't they?

And me? Well, all this confusion had turned my earlier life upside down. The facts had changed, but the memories of millions of childhood experiences were unaltered. Had it changed me? Was I the same person I was two weeks ago? There were plenty of early episodes – paddling in the river, climbing trees, snowballing on the field, messing about on the railway line. In adolescence, there was smoking and drinking, trips into Cooksley, crude encounters with various girls with occasional episodes of clumsy sex, thankful for no awkward consequences. And still later, adult life and work, with temptation lurking in every encounter away from home. All of these events now logged into memory, but sanitised and manipulated to make them more appealing, triumphs exaggerated, failures downplayed. Surely, all of these must have shaped what I had become?

When I had set out a fortnight ago, my life was solid, full of unthinking assumptions; I knew where I came from; I knew where I was going. No more. My rock-solid family foundations had crumbled.

This was too complicated. It was as if, earlier that day, the storylines of several B-movies had been condensed into a couple of hours. I needed a fag, just like the characters in the films. Deep breaths sent this drug to do its job. What was I doing? Fags killed Dad.

My body hunched up at the thought of death and shrivelled into my overcoat. I thought my memories were true, documenting my life as it rolled out. But were they? If they failed, did that mean the things they were recording failed too, disappeared from my life, robbing me of what I was and undermining what I thought I was now. I couldn't rely on memory anymore; I only had the present. Maureen and the kids were in the present. It was all I could be sure of.

We live in the present, and once a moment slides into the past, it becomes a memory. But with the passing of time, even those that take root in our minds become unreliable, condemning our lives – the ones we actually lived – to fragment and evaporate, leaving us with... what?

This book is printed on paper from sustainable sources managed under the Forest Stewardship Council (FSC) scheme.

It has been printed in the UK to reduce transportation miles and their impact upon the environment.

For every new title that Troubador publishes, we plant a tree to offset CO_2, partnering with the More Trees scheme.

MORE TREES
LET'S PLANT A BILLION TREES

For more about how Troubador offsets its environmental impact, see www.troubador.co.uk/sustainability-and-community